IN THE NURSERY

OF

MY BOOK HOUSE

EDITED BY
OLIVE BEAUPRÉ MILLER

PUBLISHERS
THE BOOK HOUSE for CHILDREN
CHICAGO

FOREWORD

By Olive Beaupré Miller

STORIES AND POEMS a child hears and reads are a most important part of the foundation upon which his life is being built. My BOOK HOUSE was definitely and consciously prepared to help educate children from the very earliest possible moment to meet life by calling out in them those qualities which make for the richest and fullest living. Therefore, at each successive and varying stage of the child's development, you will find in My BOOK HOUSE the necessary material to use in approaching the one great problem which always remains the same. That is—

How can we best assist the child to meet life and adjust himself to it?

In My BOOK HOUSE I have tried to give children the best in literature, gathered from the greatest authors of the past and present, and from our rich heritage of old folk tales, told from generation to generation in every country of the world. But I have selected these stories with care. Avoiding those tales where evil traits of character, such as lying and cheating to gain one's ends, have been made to appear good, I have chosen only those where truly desirable qualities invite the child's admiration. I have tried also to grade all this material as wisely as possible, that the child might have the right story at the right age, and to put it forth so beautifully illustrated that it would be irresistible to him. Here, in these twelve volumes, adult and child can enter, hand-in-hand, a wonderful realm of imagination and beauty, portrayed in the best literary forms of verse and prose.

My BOOK HOUSE begins with nursery rhymes, which appeal to the very young baby through their rhythm and music long before he can understand words. It is with nursery rhymes that you can first get the baby's attention and train him to listen and concentrate. Through them also and through the stories that follow them, the child is helped to learn words and increase his vocabulary, so by the time he goes to school he has the confidence that comes with the ability to express himself and his ideas.

From the nursery rhymes, My BOOK HOUSE progresses through a natural, carefully graded continuity, leading the child on gradually from the simplest stories to those that are more complex. After nursery rhymes and short poems he is given experience stories, dealing with his own experiences in the world of reality about him—what he sees on a little walk, what interests him at home, on a city street or in the country.

Following the experience stories come the repetitive stories, which have a refrain that is often repeated, like the "Not I," said the pig, "Not I," said the goose of "The Little Red Hen and the Grain of Wheat." The appeal of rhythm, music and sound is still very great to the child, as it was in the nursery rhymes, and he still has to have something short, not requiring him to concentrate for too long, as well as something very simple in thought and construction. This need is best met by the repetitive stories.

As yet the child is not ready for fairy tales. Since he is just learning the world of reality about him, he is greatly bewildered by fairies and elves and does not know where to place them in his thinking. To him an inkwell and a fairy must belong in the very same world! So I have reserved fairies, elves, giants and trolls until the child is old enough to get true enjoyment out of stories about them, which is rarely before he is six or seven years old.

Going on now to the older children, My BOOK HOUSE proceeds to the stronger and more imaginative fairy tales and to wholesome adventure stories, then on to those legends, myths and great epics which form the background of literature. And the last volume gives a story of the development of English and American literature from Chaucer down to today, presenting this background of knowledge, which boys and girls need when they enter high school, through stories of the lives of outstanding authors, told in a style to interest young people.

The permanent value of My BOOK HOUSE arises from the fact that at the time of its inception, I had no pet theory of education to advance.

No current fad, which might go out of style and be replaced by others, cramped or limited to one period my planning of these books, which were to include that basic literature which remains and will always remain the same. I was in search of fundamentals, simple fundamentals, which must remain eternally true. Chaos then existed and is, unfortunately, still permitted to exist, in the realm of reading for children. They were being given stories, ethically sound, all jumbled up with those where the ethical slant was bad, and stories for the older children were being read to the child when he was too young, overwhelming him with fright and confusion by presenting to him characters and situations far beyond his understanding at the moment. Out of this chaos I was trying to bring order, an order that could never be disturbed. So let me review those few basic principles, with which I emerged from my search and on which I built My BOOK HOUSE.

First,—To be well equipped for life, to have ideas and the ability to express them, the child needs a broad background of familiarity with the best in literature.

Second,—His stories and rhymes must be selected with care that he may absorb no distorted view of life and its actual values, but may grow up mentally clear about values and emotionally impelled to seek what is truly desirable and worthwhile in human living.

Third,—The stories and rhymes selected must be graded to the child's understanding at different periods in his growth, graded as to vocabulary, as to subject matter and as to complexity of structure and plot.

On those three simple fundamentals My BOOK HOUSE was built.

PREFACE

MOTHERS begin to sing nursery rhymes and lullabies to their babies when they are only a few weeks old. The very rhythm, music and melody of the good rhymes and lullabies soothe, quiet and train the baby. Even when the rhymes are spoken, not sung, they hold the baby's attention and he will respond to their rhythm long before he understands words. Thus the first volume of My BOOK HOUSE, "In the Nursery," is made up of a most careful selection of nursery rhymes, leading on gradually to the very simplest experience stories, demanding at each step a little more attention and concentration.

The rhymes and jingles of Old Mother Goose are, at their best, invaluable literature for old and young, never to be outgrown. But the need for a far more careful selection than is ordinarily made begins even here with these first rhymes to be given to the youngest children. So, from the pages of "In the Nursery" Old Mother Goose puts her best foot forward.

Footnotes on the historical associations of these rhymes, of no interest to the baby, prolong their use and interest for older children and even for parents. It is fascinating to learn that the queen whom Pussy Cat, Pussy Cat, saw in London was Queen Elizabeth and that Old King Cole was a third-century Celtic king in England who left his name to the town of Colchester which he seized from invading Romans. These facts are given in two of the many footnotes which place the rhymes in their original historical settings.

After these English rhymes, come about sixty pages of nursery rhymes from many countries all over the world. Such a collection has never been made before and is to be found in no other book. Moreover, I have gathered together our own American rhymes, which are here, for the first time, presented to children. From all over the United States they come—rhymes many of us knew as children but never found in a book.

There are footnotes also giving the historical associations of some of our American rhymes. They tell how Yankee Doodle arose during the American Revolution, how the Scotch, who went up into the hills of Kentucky and Tennessee, driven from their homes in the old country for their devotion to the fallen Stuart kings of England, kept alive their old ballads and in such common rhymes as "Over the hills to feed my sheep, Over the hills to Charley," retained in America their memory of their beloved young Stuart hero, Bonny Prince Charley.

After the nursery rhymes in "In the Nursery," you will find lines and verses from the great poets—Shakespeare, Keats, Burns, Tennyson, Wordsworth, Robert and Elizabeth Browning, as well as poems by Christina Rossetti, Robert Louis Stevenson, James Whitcomb Riley, Eugene Field and other poets who definitely wrote for children. There are also beautifully illustrated lines from the Bible, chosen, like the lines from the great poets, to give only that little flash of poetic imagery which will appeal to a small child and is within the scope of his present understanding and feelings.

Following these rhymes, comes that valuable section of prose material which is generally called experience stories. These stories, very short and simple, deal with the baby's own experience, his own sense perceptions, the activity of his body. They tell how he gets dressed, what he sees on a little walk, what interests him at home, at play, in the country or in the city, what he hears, what he sees, what he tastes, what he smells. This kind of story is the first prose to which a child will listen with interest and it not only broadens the scope of the things he notices in the world about him, but prepares him for the slightly more complicated repetitive stories in Volume Two.

Necessary though they are in filling in for the child this gap between rhymes and prose, experience stories can scarcely be called literature, though it is interesting to note that one of our greatest modern novelists, Pearl Buck, did not disdain to use her great talents in writing such a simple story—"What the Children Do in Summer"—which is given on page 212. In addition to her lively little picture of child life, I have chosen only those experience stories by the best authors, stories which have a fine rhythm in their prose and a real feeling for the subject portrayed. Moreover, wherever possible, I have made these stories a connecting link with literature by giving along with them a poem on the subject of the story. When the child hears the story about rain in "The Big Umbrella and the Little Rubbers," he will listen eagerly at its conclusion to Robert Louis Stevenson's poem, "Rain." When he hears how all the clothes on the clothesline dance in the wind, Christina Rossetti's "Who has Seen the Wind?" seems to him like part of that same story. And the tale of the little boy who went out into the snow with his mother to make a snow man runs naturally into the beautiful lines by James Stephens—

"In the winter time we go
Walking in the fields of snow."

Thus even in this stage of his growth the child need not be separated from literature.

"In the Nursery" ends with the story of Mary and the Christ-Child, told in verse as being better suited to the young child. And where the child is too young to hear this whole story, the illustrations can be used to tell him as much as he can grasp. A child of two and a half will understand the picture on page 221 of the baby in the manger with all the animals around if these details are pointed out to him. He will understand that it is the baby's birthday, since he has passed his own second birthday, the first birthday a child recognizes as such and associates with presents. Then if the picture on page 219 is used, he will understand that the men on camels are bringing the baby birthday presents and that the star in the sky is leading them to where he is. Lastly the picture on page 223, shows him how the men arrived with their gifts and gave them to the baby. Ingenious parents may also find ways to use others of these illustrations for their youngest children. But by the time the child is five he is usually ready for this story as a whole.

CONTENTS

THE world is so full
     Of a number of things,
I'm sure we should all
Be as happy as kings.
          —Robert Louis Stevenson

17

English Nursery Rhymes

DANCE, little Baby, dance up high!
    Never mind, Baby, Mother is by
Crow and caper, caper and crow,
    There, little Baby, there you go!
Up to the ceiling, down to the ground,
    Backwards and forwards,
                    round and round,
Dance, little Baby, and Mother will sing
    With a merry carol, ding! ding! ding!

SEE-SAW, sacaradown,
    Which is the way to London town?
One foot up, the other down,
    This is the way to London town.

ROCK-A-BYE, baby,
    Thy cradle is green;
Father's a nobleman,
    Mother's a queen;
And Betty's a lady,
    And wears a gold ring,
And Johnny's a drummer,
    And drums for the king.

PAT-A-CAKE, pat-a-cake, baker's man!
　Make me a cake as fast as you can;
Prick it, and pat it, and mark it with T,
　And put it in the oven for Tommy and me.

HOW many days has my baby to play?
　Saturday, Sunday, Monday —
Tuesday, Wednesday, Thursday, Friday,
　Saturday, Sunday, Monday.

THIS little pig went to market;
　This little pig stayed at home;
　　This little pig had roast beef;
This little pig had none;
　This little pig said, "Wee, wee, wee!
　　I can't find my way home!"

SLEEP, baby, sleep,
  Our cottage vale is deep;
The little lamb is on the green,
With woolly fleece so soft and clean.
  Sleep, baby, sleep.

OH, here's a leg for a stocking,
  And here's a foot for a shoe,
And he has a kiss for his daddy,
  And two for his mammy, I trow.

JOHNNY shall have a new bonnet,
  And Johnny shall go to the fair,
And Johnny shall have a blue ribbon
  To tie up his bonny brown hair.

"BOW-wow," says the dog;
    "Mew, mew," says the cat;
"Grunt, grunt," goes the hog;
    And "Squeak!" goes the rat.
"Chirp, chirp," says the sparrow;
"Caw, caw," says the crow;
"Quack, quack," says the duck;
    And the cuckoo you know.

So with sparrows and cuckoos,
With rats and with dogs,
With ducks and with crows,
With cats and with hogs!
A fine song I've made
To please you, my dear,
And if it's well sung,
'Twill be charming to hear.

H ICKORY, dickory, dock! The mouse ran up the clock;
The clock struck one, the mouse ran down,
Hickory, dickory, dock!*

G OOSEY, Goosey, Gander,
Whither shall I wander?
Upstairs and downstairs,
And in my lady's chamber.

H EY diddle diddle,
The cat and the fiddle!
The cow jumped over the moon;
The little dog laughed
To see such sport,
And the dish ran away with the spoon.

*So old are many English nursery rhymes that some, like *Hickory Dickory Dock*, keep the memory of the Celtic language,
spoken long before English in England. Old shepherds still count their sheep *hovera, covera, dik*, instead of eight, nine, ten.

OLD Mother Goose, when
 She wanted to wander,
Would ride through the air
 On a very fine gander.

Mother Goose had a house,
 'Twas built in a wood,
Where an owl at the door
 For sentinel stood.*

LITTLE Robin Redbreast
 Sat upon a rail.
Niddle-naddle went his head,
 Wiggle-waggle went his tail.

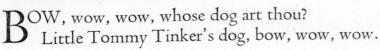

BOW, wow, wow, whose dog art thou?
 Little Tommy Tinker's dog, bow, wow, wow.

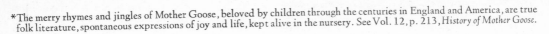

*The merry rhymes and jingles of Mother Goose, beloved by children through the centuries in England and America, are true folk literature, spontaneous expressions of joy and life, kept alive in the nursery. See Vol. 12, p. 213, *History of Mother Goose.*

HICKETY, pickety, my black hen,
    She lays eggs for gentlemen;
Gentlemen come every day
    To see what my black hen doth lay.

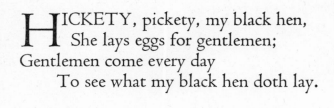

RIDE away, ride away,
    Johnny shall ride,
And he shall have pussy-cat
    Tied to one side;
He shall have little dog
    Tied to the other,
And Johnny shall ride
    To see his grandmother.

DICKERY, dickery, dare,
    The pig flew up in the air;
The man in brown soon brought him down,
    Dickery,
        dickery,
            dare.

ONCE I saw a little bird
    Come hop, hop, hop;
So I cried, "Little bird,
    Will you stop, stop, stop?"
I was going to the window
    To say, "How do you do?"
But he shook his little tail,
    And away he flew.

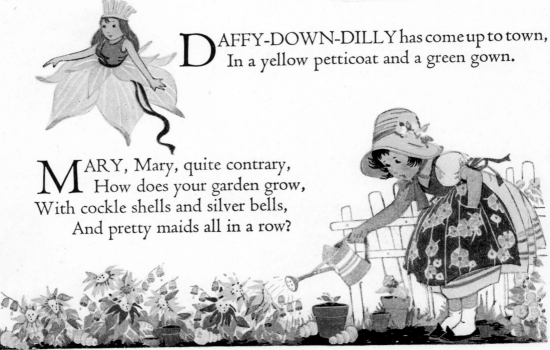

DAFFY-DOWN-DILLY has come up to town,
    In a yellow petticoat and a green gown.

MARY, Mary, quite contrary,
    How does your garden grow,
With cockle shells and silver bells,
    And pretty maids all in a row?

THERE was an old woman of Harrow,
  Who visited in a wheelbarrow,
And her servant before
  Knocked loud at each door
To announce the old woman of Harrow.

LUCY Locket lost her pocket;
  Kittie Fisher found it;
There was not a penny in it,
  But a ribbon round it!

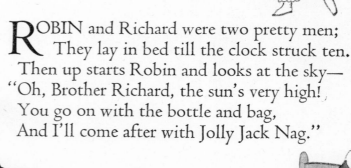

ROBIN and Richard were two pretty men;
  They lay in bed till the clock struck ten.
Then up starts Robin and looks at the sky—
"Oh, Brother Richard, the sun's very high!
You go on with the bottle and bag,
And I'll come after with Jolly Jack Nag."

I HAD a little husband no bigger than my thumb;
I put him in a pint pot and there I bade him drum;
I bought a little handkerchief to wipe his little nose,
And a pair of little garters to tie his little hose.
I bought a little horse that galloped up and down;
I bridled him and saddled him and sent him out of town.*

THERE was an old woman
Lived under a hill;
And if she's not gone,
She lives there still.

A PIE sat on a pear tree,
A pie sat on a pear tree,
A pie sat on a pear tree,
Heigh O, heigh O, heigh O!

Once so merrily hopped she,
Twice so merrily hopped she,
Thrice so merrily hopped she,
Heigh O, heigh O, heigh O!

*I Had a Little Husband celebrates Tom Thumb, the dwarf of Scandinavian legend, later said to have lived at King Arthur's court in England, and to have been buried in Lincoln Cathedral. Visitors were shown his little gravestone.

RIDE a cock-horse to Banbury Cross,
    To see a fine lady upon a white horse;
Rings on her fingers, and bells on her toes,
    She shall make music wherever she goes.

HIPPETY hop to the barber shop,
    To get a stick of candy,
One for you and one for me,
    And one for Sister Mandy.

WEE Willie Winkie
    Runs through the town,
Upstairs and downstairs
    In his nightgown,
Rapping at the window,
    Crying through the lock,
"Are the children in their beds,
    For it's now eight o'clock?"

BAA, baa, black sheep, have you any wool?
    "Yes, Sir, yes, Sir, three bags full;
One for my master, one for my dame,
    And one for the little boy who lives in the lane."

THERE was a piper had a cow,
    And he had naught to give her;
He took his pipes and played a tune,
    And bade the cow consider.
The cow considered very well,
    And gave the piper a penny,
And bade him play the other tune,
    "Corn rigs are bonny."

AS I went to Bonner,
    I met a pig
        Without a wig,
Upon my word and honor.

SMILING girls, rosy boys,
  Come and buy my little toys,
Monkeys made of ginger bread,
  And sugar horses painted red.

THERE was an old man
  And he had a calf,
  And that's half;
He took him out of the stall
And put him on the wall,
  And that's all.

UP in the green orchard there is a green tree,
  The finest of pippins that ever you see;
The apples are ripe, and ready to fall,
  And Reuben and Robin shall gather them all.

BLOW, wind, blow, and go, mill, go!
That the miller may grind his corn;
That the baker may take it,
And into rolls make it,
And send us some hot in the morn.

POLLY, put the kettle on,
Polly, put the kettle on,
Polly, put the kettle on;
We'll all have tea.
Sukey, take it off again,
Sukey, take it off again,
Sukey, take it off again;
They're all gone away.

SING, sing!—What shall I sing?
The Cat's run away with the Pudding Bag String.
Do, do!—What shall I do?
The Cat has bitten it quite in two.

LITTLE Bo-Peep has lost her sheep,
    And can't tell where to find them.
Leave them alone, and they'll come home,
    Bringing their tails behind them.*

HERE am I, little jumping Joan;
    When nobody's with me,
        I'm always alone.

COCK-a-doodle-doo!
    My dame has lost her shoe;
My master's lost his fiddling stick
    And doesn't know what to do!
Cock-a-doodle-doo!
    What is my dame to do?
Till master finds his fiddling stick,
    She'll dance without her shoe.
Cock-a-doodle-doo!
    My dame has found her shoe,
And master's found his fiddling stick,
    Sing cock-a-doodle-doo!

*Bo-Peep, a rhyme of England's sheep farms and great wool trade, was known in 1364, when Alice Causton, for giving short measure in ale, was condemned to "play bo-peep through a pillory." Shakespeare mentions Bo-Peep in *King Lear*.

LITTLE Boy Blue, come blow your horn;
　　The sheep's in the meadow, the cow's in the corn.
Where's the little boy that looks after the sheep?
　　He's under the hay-cock, fast asleep.

HANDY-SPANDY, Jack-a-dandy,
　　Loves plum cake and sugar candy.
He bought some at a baker's shop,
　　And pleased, away ran, hop, hop, hop.

TO market, to market, to buy a fat pig;
　Home again, home again, dancing a jig.
To market, to market, to buy a fat hog;
　Home again, home again, jiggety-jog.
To market, to market, to buy a plum bun;
　Home again, home again, market is done.

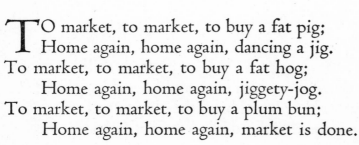

To Market, to Market is the English version of the rhyme used when fathers trot children on their knees. See the Norse
Ride Away on page 60, Swiss Jokeli, page 66, Spanish To Bethlehem, page 65, and Penna. Dutch Ride, Ride a Horsey, page 116.

TOM, Tom, the piper's son,
  Learned to play when he was young,
But all the tune that he could play,
Was "Over the hills and far away,
Over the hills and a great way off,
And the wind will blow my top-knot off."

Now Tom with his pipe did make such a noise,
That he surely pleased both the girls and the boys,
They all stood still, for to hear him play,
"Over the hills and far away."

Tom with his pipe did play with such skill
That those who heard him could never keep still;
Whenever they heard him, they began to dance;
Even pigs on their hind legs would after him prance.

Tom, Tom is a song of about 1745, when Scotch Highlanders piped *Over the Hills and Far Away* because their adored Bonny Prince Charley, young Pretender to the throne of England, was forced to live far away in Europe.

I SAW a ship a-sailing,
   A-sailing on the sea;
And it was full of pretty things
   For baby and for me!

There were comfits in the cabin,
   And apples in the hold;
The sails were all of velvet,
   And the masts of beaten gold.

The four-and-twenty sailors
   That stood between the decks,
Were four-and-twenty white mice,
   With chains about their necks.

The Captain was a duck,
   With a packet on his back;
And when the ship began to move,
   The Captain said, "Quack! Quack!"

PETER, Peter, pumpkin eater,
 Had a wife and couldn't keep her;
He put her in a pumpkin shell,
 And there he kept her very well.

A ROBIN and a robin's son
 Once went to town to buy a bun.
They couldn't decide on plum or plain
 And so they went back home again.

PUSSY sits beside the fire,
 How can she be fair?
In comes the little dog,
 "Pussy, are you there:
So, so, dear Mistress Pussy,
 Pray how do you do?"
"I thank you, little Doggie,
 I fare as well as you."

WHAT'S the news of the day,
　　Good neighbor, I pray?
They say the balloon
　　Has gone up to the moon.

DIDDLE, diddle, dumpling, my son John
　　Went to bed with his breeches on;
One shoe off and the other shoe on,
　　Diddle, diddle, dumpling, my son John.

I HAD a little nut tree, and nothing would it bear
　Save a silver nutmeg and a golden pear.
The King of Spain's daughter came to visit me,
And all for the sake of my little nut tree.
I skipped over water, I danced over sea,
And all the birds in the air couldn't catch me.

Old Mother Hubbard

OLD Mother Hubbard went to the cupboard,
　To get her poor doggie a bone,
But when she got there, the cupboard was bare,
And so the poor doggie had none.

She went to the Hatter's to buy him a hat,
And when she came back he was feeding the cat.

She went to the Tailor's to buy him a coat,
　And when she came back he was riding the goat.

She went to the Barber's to buy him a wig,
And when she came back he was dancing a jig.

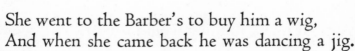

The dame made a curtsy, the dog made a bow,
The dame said, "Your servant"; the dog said, "Bow-wow."

BOYS and girls, come out to play;
  The moon doth shine as bright as day.
Come with a whoop, come with a call,
  Come with a good will, or don't you come at all!
Up with the ladder and down the wall,
  A halfpenny roll will serve us all.
You find milk and I'll find flour,
  And we'll have a pudding in less than an hour.

FOUR-AND-TWENTY tailors went to catch a snail;
  The best man amongst them durst not touch her tail;
She put out her horns, like a little Kyloe cow.
Run, tailors, run, or she'll butt you all just now.

JACK, be nimble,
    Jack, be quick;
Jack, jump over
    The candlestick.

LITTLE Miss Muffet
　　Sat on a tuffet,
Eating her curds and whey;
　　Along came a spider,
　　And sat down beside her,
And frightened Miss Muffet away.

JACK and Jill went up the hill
　　To fetch a pail of water;
Jack fell down and broke his crown
And Jill came tumbling after.*

LITTLE King Boggin built a fine hall,
　　Pie crust and pastry crust, that was the wall;
The windows were made of black puddings and white
　　And slated with pancakes—you ne'er saw the like.

*Jack and Jill is as old as the Younger Edda (Norse, 13th Century) which tells how two children, Hjuki and Bill, carrying a bucket of water, were taken up to the sky. Peasants still see them in the moon.

THE King of France went up the hill
    With twenty-thousand men;
The King of France came down the hill
    And ne'er went up again.

LITTLE Nanny Etticoat
    In a white petticoat
And a red nose—
The longer she stands,
The shorter she grows.

THERE was an old woman tossed up in a basket,
    Seventy times as high as the moon,
And where she was going, I couldn't but ask it;
    For in her hand she carried a broom.
"Old woman, old woman, old woman," quoth I,
    "Whither, Oh whither, Oh whither so high?"
"To sweep the cobwebs out of the sky!
    "And I'll be with you by and by."*

*With this rhyme street crowds in 15th-century England mocked King Henry V when he set out to conquer France, calling him an old woman setting out on an absurd and impossible undertaking. The rhyme above ridicules the French King.

LITTLE Tommy Tucker
    Sings for his supper.
What shall we give him?
    White bread and butter.
How shall he cut it
    Without e'er a knife?
How shall he marry
    Without e'er a wife?

ONE misty, moisty morning,
    When cloudy was the weather.
I chanced to meet an old man
    Clothed all in leather.

He began to compliment
    And I began to grin,
With "How do you do?" and "How do you do?"
    And "How do you do, again?"

THE cock's on the housetop blowing his horn;
    The bull's in the barn a-threshing of corn;
The maids in the meadows are making of hay;
    The ducks in the rain are swimming away.

THERE was an Old Woman
Who lived in a shoe;
She had so many children
She didn't know what to do.

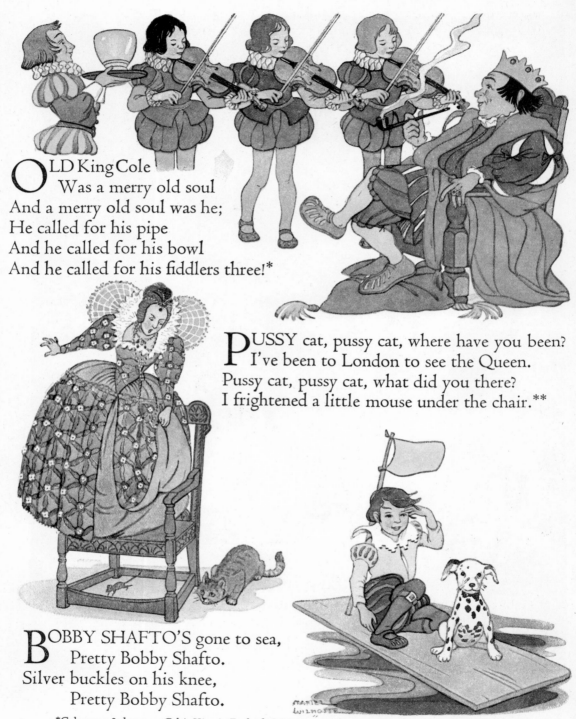

OLD King Cole
Was a merry old soul
And a merry old soul was he;
He called for his pipe
And he called for his bowl
And he called for his fiddlers three!*

PUSSY cat, pussy cat, where have you been?
I've been to London to see the Queen.
Pussy cat, pussy cat, what did you there?
I frightened a little mouse under the chair.**

BOBBY SHAFTO'S gone to sea,
Pretty Bobby Shafto.
Silver buckles on his knee,
Pretty Bobby Shafto.

*Cole was a 3rd-century Celtic King in England. Seizing a camp from invading Romans, he named it *Colchester* or *Cole's Camp*. Today, as a city, it still bears his name. **The Queen seen by Pussy in London was Elizabeth.

BAT, bat, come under my hat,
  And I'll give you a slice of bacon;
And when I bake,
I'll give you a cake,
If I am not mistaken.

HECTOR Protector was dressed all in green;
  Hector Protector was sent to the Queen;
    The Queen did not like him,
    No more did the King;
So Hector Protector was sent back again.*

WILLIE boy, Willie boy,
  Where are you going?
Oh, let us go with you,
  This sunshiny day.

I'm going to the meadow,
  To see them a-mowing,
I'm going to help the girls
  Turn the new hay.

*The Hector Protector, sent home in disgrace by the King, was Oliver Cromwell, Lord High
Protector of England, naturally no favorite with kings since he dethroned Charles I, in 1649.

AS Tommy Snooks and Bessie Brooks
Were walking out one Sunday,
Said Tommy Snooks to Bessie Brooks,
"Tomorrow will be Monday!"

HUMPTY DUMPTY sat on a wall,
Humpty Dumpty had a great fall.
All the king's horses, and all the king's men,
Couldn't put Humpty Dumpty together again.*

MY lady Wind, my lady Wind,
Went round about the house to find
A chink to get her foot in;
She tried the keyhole in the door;
She tried the crevice in the floor,
And drove the chimney soot in.

*Though 13th-century English parents told children Humpty Dumpty was an egg, they really meant Humpty Dumpty whose fall could never be repaired as a jibe at King John, the tyrant, from whom they forced *Magna Charta*, their charter of liberty.

46

BILLY, Billy, come and play,
　While the sun shines bright as day.
Yes, my Polly, so I will,
For I love to please you still.

Billy, Billy, have you seen
Sam and Betsy on the green?
Yes, my Poll, I saw them pass,
Skipping o'er the new-mown grass.

Billy, Billy, come along,
And I will sing a pretty song.
Oh, then, Polly, I'll make haste;
Not one moment will I waste.

PEASE-porridge hot, pease-porridge cold,
　Pease-porridge in the pot, nine days old.
Some like it hot, some like it cold,
　Some like it in the pot, nine days old.

RUB-A-DUB-DUB, three men in a tub,
And who do you think they be?
The butcher, the baker, the candlestick maker,
And all of them gone to sea.

LITTLE Jack Horner
Sat in the corner,
Eating his Christmas pie;
He put in his thumb,
And pulled out a plum,
And said, "What a good boy am I!"*

*Jack Horner was a man who really lived in 16th-century England, and the plum he pulled out was a fine estate which he got out of lands seized by Henry VIII from the church. See Vol. 12, p. 213, *The Interesting History of Old Mother Goose.*

SING a song of sixpence,
   A pocket full of rye;
Four and twenty blackbirds,
   Baked in a pie.

When the pie was opened,
   The birds began to sing;
Wasn't that a dainty dish,
   To set before the King?

The King was in the counting house,
   Counting out his money;
The Queen was in the parlor,
   Eating bread and honey.

The Maid was in the garden,
   Hanging out the clothes;
Down came a blackbird,
   And snapped off her nose!

Sing a Song of Sixpence was well-known in England in the 16th Century. In the days of Shakespeare and Queen Elizabeth, it was already an old favorite.

SIMPLE SIMON met a pie-man,
　　Going to the fair.
Said Simple Simon to the pie-man:
　　"Let me taste your ware."

Said the pie-man to Simple Simon:
　　"Show me first your penny."
Said Simple Simon to the pie-man:
　　"Indeed, I haven't any."

Simple Simon went a-fishing,
　　For to catch a whale;
But all the water he could find
　　Was in his mother's pail!*

THERE was an owl lived in an oak,
　　Wisky, wasky, weedle;
And all the words he ever spoke,
　　Were, "Fiddle, faddle, feedle."

*Simple Simon, a rhyme of Queen Elizabeth's time (16th Cent.) comes, like many English nursery rhymes, from one of those old chap-books sold by peddlers at country fairs. Spain and Spanish-American countries have similar rhymes of Simple Simon.

THERE were two blackbirds
   Sitting on a hill,
The one named Jack,
And the other named Jill.
    Fly away, Jack!
    Fly away, Jill!
    Come again, Jack!
    Come again, Jill!

MY maid Mary she minds the dairy,
   While I go a-hoeing and mowing each morn;
Gaily run the reel and the little spinning-wheel,
   While I am a-singing and mowing my corn.

SEE-SAW, Margery Daw,
   Jenny shall have a new master.
She shall have but a penny a day,
   Because she can't work any faster.

GREAT A, little a, bouncing B,
The Cat's in the cupboard and she can't see.

THERE was a monkey
climbed a tree;
When he fell down,
then down fell he.

A LITTLE cock sparrow sat on a green tree,
And he chirruped, he chirruped, so merry was he.
A little cock sparrow sat on a green tree,
And he chirruped, he chirruped, so merry was he.

Three Little Kittens

THREE little kittens lost their mittens,
And they began to cry:
"Oh! Mother dear,
We sadly fear
That we have lost our mittens."

"Lost your mittens,
You careless kittens!
Then you shall have no pie!"
"Mia-ow, mia-ow, mia-ow!"
"No, you shall have no pie!"
"Mia-ow, mia-ow, mia-ow!"

The three little kittens found their mittens,
And they began to cry:
"Oh! Mother dear,
See here, see here!
See, we have found our mittens!"

"What, found your mittens,
You good little kittens!
Then you shall have some pie."
"Purr-r, purr-r, purr-r,
Oh, thank you for the pie!
Purr-r, purr-r, purr-r."

G AY go up and gay go down,
   To ring the bells of London town.

"Oranges and lemons,"
   Say the bells of St. Clement's.

"You owe me ten shillin's,"
   Say the bells of St. Helen's.

   "When will you pay me?"
      Say the bells of Old Bailey.

   "When I grow rich,"
      Say the bells of Shoreditch.

T HERE was a crow sat on a stone;
   When he was gone, then there was none.

T HERE was a horse went to the mill;
   When he went on, he stood not still.

HOW many miles to Babylon?
    Three-score and ten.
Will we be there by candlelight?
    Yes, and back again.

Open your gates and let us go through.
Not without a beck and a boo.
There's a beck and there's a boo;
Open your gates and let us go through.

BIRDS of a feather flock together,
    And so will pigs and swine;
Rats and mice will have their choice,
    And so will I have mine.

LITTLE maid, pretty maid, whither goest thou?
　Down in the forest to milk my cow.
Shall I go with thee? No, not now;
When I send for thee, then come thou.

LAVENDER'S blue, dilly, dilly,
　Lavender's green;
When I'm a king, dilly, dilly,
You shall be queen!

LITTLE girl, little girl, where have you been?
　Gathering roses to give to the Queen.
Little girl, little girl, what gave she you?
　She gave me a diamond as big as my shoe.

THERE are twelve months in all the year,
As I hear many say,
But the merriest month in all the year
Is the merry month of May!

—*Old English Ballad*

IN Spring the birds do sing,
They do, they do!
They sing;
"Cuckoo, jug-jug, pu-we, to-wit-to-woo!"

WHEN woods awake and trees are green
And leaves are large and long,
'Tis merry to walk in the forest fair
And hear the small birds' song.

—*Old English Ballad*

While 11th-century nobles sang of knightly deeds, common people in England wove their own merry ballads, pouring out their joy in life, their love of "pretty fair maids," small birds and forests green, the "red rose" and blooming things.

Welsh and Scotch Rhymes

DAME Durden kept five serving maids
    To carry the milking pail;
She also kept five lab'ring men
To use the spade and flail;
'Twas Moll and Bet and Doll and Kate
And Dorothy Draggle-tail;
And John and Dick and Joe and Jack
And Humphrey with his flail!

—*Welsh*

DANCE to your daddie,
    My bonnie laddie,
Dance to your daddie, my bonnie lamb!
    And ye'll get a fishie
    In a little dishie,
Ye'll get a fishie when the boat comes home!

—*Scotch*

Rhymes from Ireland

O 'TWAS on a bright mornin' in summer,
   When I first heard her voice singin' low,
And I said to the colleen beside me:
"Who's the pretty girl milkin' the cow?"

D OWN in a cottage lives Weaver John,
   And a happy old John is he;
Maud is the name of his dear old dame,
And a blessed old dame is she.

Whickity, whackity, click and clack,
How the shuttles do glance and ring!
Here they go, there they go, forth and back,
And a whackity song they sing.

Norse Nursery Rhymes

RIDE, ride away,*
   Our horsey's Dapple Gray,
And Baby's on his back,
O where shall he ride today?

   To the King's Castle
   And knock, knock, knock!
   Nobody home!   Nobody home!

      Only two little dogs are there,
      Lying together under the chair,
      One little dog says, "Woof!"
      The other says, "Woof, woof, woof!"
                        —Ride, ride, ranke

THE squirrel went out to cut the hay;
   Did you hear how he chattered and chattered away?
The blackbird raked, the crow pulled the load,
And pussy-cat drove the cart way down the road!
            —Ekorn, han gik ut i enga og slog

THE HOLLINGS

*Ride Away is used in Norway when fathers ride children on their feet. Most countries have such rhymes.   See the Swiss *Jokeli*, p. 66; the Penna. Dutch *Ride, Ride a Horsey*, p. 116; the Spanish *To Bethlehem*, p. 65; and the English rhymes pages 28 and 33.

REINAR was watching his cows
  In sunshine and in rain;
Berries and berries he ate, and berries and berries again.
Always he sat on a hill and sang a little song;
And he was just as happy as the day is long.
—*Reinar skulde ut aa gjaete*

ROW, row! A-fishing we'll go!
  How many fishes have you, Joe?
One for my father, one for my mother,
One for my sister, one for my brother,
And one for the little fisher boy!
—*Ro, ro til fiskeskjaer*

THE HOLLINGS

Italian Nursery Rhymes

IF I could walk for two weeks and a day,
   And go where the hills meet the sky,
I think I'd find children who play in the clouds,
And who can really fly!

—Lombardy

LITTLE Peppino, the shepherd boy,
   Sings to the sheep in the meadow green,
But when the hungry wolf comes out,
The shepherd's dog goes after him!

—Campania

THE HOLLINGS

These rhymes were brought from Italy by Arturo Fallico.

MARIO, Marietta, and Vanno
Went to the Fair today;
They each brought back a pumpkin,
But I stayed home to play.
—Sicily

LITTLE Beppo Pippo
Was a sailor-man;
He made himself a boat
And sailed it in a pan!
—From an old Neapolitan "sillabario"

GIUSEPPI, the cobbler, makes my shoes;
He pounds them, rap, rap, rap!
He makes them small, he makes them big,
And ever he pounds, tap, tap!
—Tuscany

63

Spanish Nursery Rhymes

FIVE little chicks
Does my aunt keep;
One jumps;
One pecks;
One sings,
"Cheep, cheep, cheep!"

   —*Cinco pollitos tiene mi tía*

PUSSY, Kittie
Went to the square;
There he bought a fish;
Straight away he ate it
Off a pretty dish.
Shoo, shoo, little Kittie!

   —*Mizo, gato*

WHO'S on the roof, pit-a-pat, pit-a-pat?
Only the yellow pussy cat.
Pray what is she doing now?
Miaow! Miaow! Miaow!
Tell me how does pussy scratch?
Scritch-scratch! Scritch-scratch!

   —*¿Quién está en el tejado?*

64

GET up, little horsey,
  Go to Bethlehem;
Tomorrow there's a feast day,
Next day feast again!

Get up, little horsey,
To the fair in town;
Do not stumble, horsey,
Or I'll tumble down!

Get up, little horsey,
To Bethlehem go straight;
Hurry, hurry, hurry,
Or we'll be too late!

Get up, little horsey,
To Bethlehem with you;
There we'll see the Virgin
And the Christ-child, too.

—*Arre, caballito vamos á Belén*

THE HOLLINGS

Swiss Nursery Rhymes

JOKELI, Jokeli, can you ride—
    Trot, trot, trot?
Aye, over every green mountain side—
    Trot, trot, trot!
Then go, pony, go, with a clickety clack!
Bang! You've thrown Jokeli off your back!*
       —*Jokeli kasch au ryte?*

O WILL you shoe our pony, pray?
    To Basel we would ride away!
What shall he carry on his back?
A cookie in a paper sack,
A little cheese, some curds and whey,
And we'll come back tomorrow day!
    —*Mer wänd das Ressli bschlo loh?*

*This is the Swiss version of the rhyme used when a father trots his child on his foot.

66

THE roosters at the old
       Crown Inn
Are angry, one and all,
When a fine rooster comes from
      another yard
    To pay their hens a call!
        —*In Basel in der Krone*

CHIMNEY sweep, you black man,
   You've sooty clothes tonight.
All the washwomen from Paris
Can never wash them white!
    —*Kemifeger*

IT'S raining! It's raining!
  It's pouring from the sky!
Let's crawl inside this barrel
And that will keep us dry!
     —*S' rägelet und s' tröpfelet*

South American Rhymes

THE toads in the lake,
When it rains pitter-pat—
Some ask for a cap
And some ask for a hat.
—*Los sapos en la laguna*

MR. Toad set out on a journey,
His donkeys each bearing a pack.
Said Mrs. Toad, "My darling,
When are you coming back?"
—*El sapo estaba de viaje*

WHEN Mrs. Bird wants Mr. Bird
To get dressed up for church,
She starches his white pantaloons
And irons his Sunday shirt!
—*Cuando la perica quiere*

These favorite rhymes of children in Colombia, South America, were translated from the Spanish of Don Antonio José Restrepo (1855-1933), one of the best-known Colombian poets.

RIGHT out in our barnyard
  Two big bulls fought today;
One of the bulls was red,
And the other one ran away!
  —*En el corral de mi casa*

WHEN I see a lady, a very pretty lady,
  I turn my head and look at her just
    like that;
I smile at her politely and pass her by a-singing,
I pass her by a-singing and I lift my hat.
  —*Cuando veo una bonita*

Mexican Rhymes

COME, let's go to Sant' Anita;
Come, let's go and there we'll find
Wagons doing all the pulling
With the oxen hitched behind!

—*Vámonos por Santa Anita*

CHINK, chink, chocket,
Pennies in my pocket!
And little cakes
To buy, to buy,
For this one and another!
I'll buy the best for Mother!

THE HOLLINGS

The verses, on pages 70 and 71, excepting the first one above, were
collected in Mexico by Frances Toor, Editor of *Mexican Folkways*.

70

I'M a little Indian;
I stand here at the gate,
A-selling jars and beaters
for your chocolate!
—*Yo soy una inditararara*

THIS one stole an egg,
this one fried it,
this one salted it,
this one ate it,
and this old dog went
and tattled all about it!*

THIS little ant worked with might
and main,
Bringing in wood till it started
to rain.
Then to his ant-hill off he hurried,
Into his little house he scurried.

*This is the Mexican version of the English rhyme *This Little Pig Went to Market* used when the mother counts off the baby's toes.

71

Polish Rhymes

BIG clock—tick, tock!
　Little watch—tick, tick, tick!
Big bells—bim, bam, bam!
Little bells, hark,
Like the lark—
Tinkle, tinkle, tinkle, tinkle!

GURGLE, water, gurgle
　In a covered well—
Why does water gurgle?
'Cause it's water in a well!

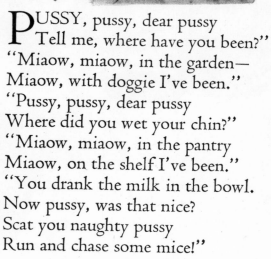

PUSSY, pussy, dear pussy
　Tell me, where have you been?"
"Miaow, miaow, in the garden—
Miaow, with doggie I've been."
"Pussy, pussy, dear pussy
Where did you wet your chin?"
"Miaow, miaow, in the pantry
Miaow, on the shelf I've been."
"You drank the milk in the bowl.
Now pussy, was that nice?
Scat you naughty pussy
Run and chase some mice!"

These rhymes were collected in Poland by C. Stanley Zalewski.

A WOMAN had a rooster, a rooster, a rooster,
  She put him in a shoe, in a shoe, in a shoe.
O my little rooster, rooster, rooster,
How do you like it in the shoe, in the shoe?

A woman had a turkey, a turkey, a turkey,
She put him in a sack, in a sack, in a sack.
O my little turkey, turkey, turkey,
How do you like it in the sack, in the sack?

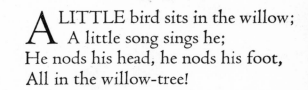

A LITTLE bird sits in the willow;
  A little song sings he;
He nods his head, he nods his foot,
All in the willow-tree!

D IDDLE, diddle on a bass fiddle,
  Tommy Cat plays all day.
Says Pussy-cat Bess, "I must confess
'Tis wondrous well you play!"

Swedish Rhymes

PEEKABOO, I see you!
　　Tra-la-la-la-la!
If I see you, then you see me,
If you see me, then I see you,
　　Tra-la-la-la-la!*

THERE were two little boys
　　A-playing in the snow.
They took their little sleds
And they slid to and fro!

　　　　—*Där gingo två gossar i snöden*

HOP, Mother Annika!　Hop, Mother Annika!
　　See your little girl dancing!
Dance when you're little, dance with a will!
Then when you're big you'll be dancing still!

　　　　—*Hopp, mor Annika!*

I See You is an old Swedish dance song and peekaboo game generally played
outdoors behind trees. These rhymes are known and loved by every child in Sweden.

OTTO would a-riding go,
So he harnessed up a crow.
Could he drive it? No, no, no!
Otto humped and bumped around
And Otto tumbled on the ground!

I TOOK a walk one evening
All in a meadow sweet,
And there I chanced that evening
A little girl to meet.
She said, "Good evening" to me,
She gave to me her hand;
We sang and played together
In the fresh green meadow land.
—*Jag gick mej ut en afton*

EVERYONE'S glad in our city today;
There's no one who is not happy and gay
When grandpa and grandma and grandchildren eight
Come riding along through the wide city gate.
—*Sig gladde av hjärtat vår nyfikna stad*

Good phonograph records reproduce with much spirit these old Swedish folk
songs as well as those from France, Germany, Bohemia, and other countries.

Chinese Nursery Rhymes

OLD Mother Wind,
   Come this way,
And make our baby
Cool to-day.

THERE was an old woman,
   As I have heard tell,
She went to sell pie,
   But her pie would not sell.

She hurried back home,
   But her door-step was high,
She stumbled and fell
   And a dog ate her pie.

From *Chinese Mother Goose Rhymes*, translated by Isaac T. Headland, published by Fleming II. Revell Company.

THE mouse climbed up the candlestick,
To steal the tallow from the wick.
When he got up he couldn't get down,
He called so loud he waked the town.
He called for the cat, but the cat wouldn't come,
So he called for his mother to take him home.

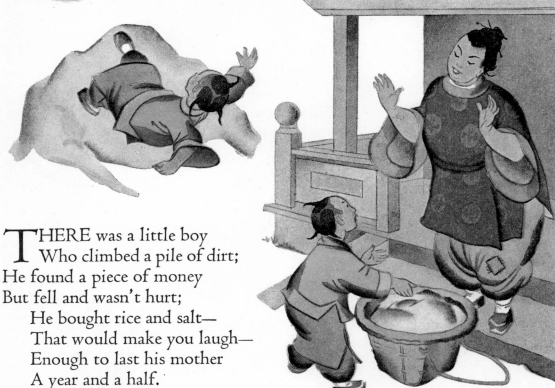

THERE was a little boy
Who climbed a pile of dirt;
He found a piece of money
But fell and wasn't hurt;
He bought rice and salt—
That would make you laugh—
Enough to last his mother
A year and a half.

From *Chinese Rhymes for Children*, translated by Isaac T. Headland, published by Fleming H. Revell Company.

A Japanese Lullaby

SLEEP, my baby! Sleep my baby!
  Where is Nursie gone?
Away way over the mountain-tops
Nursie has gone home.
And from her little village
What will Nursie bring?

A drum, rub-a-dub, and a flute of bamboo
A tumble-down dolly that stands straight for you
And a small paper dog on a string!

East Indian Rhymes

THE Rajah went to Delhi,
    The road was laid with mats;
    The Rajah went to Delhi,
       And brought back seven cats.

Through the jungle an old woman wandered,
Her journey was crooked and far;
So being afraid of all wild jungle folk,
She rolled in a large earthen jar.

    Cried Gedar, the Jackal, "Where go you?"
    Cried Lomri, the Fox, "Where from?"
    But all that the bouncing jar would say,
    Was "Thum-ak-a, Thum-ak-a, Thum!"

These verses from the Hindustani were translated into English by Mrs. Rockwell
Clancy whose Indian nurse sang them to her when she was a child in Northern India.

American Indian Songs

LITTLE good baby,
  he-ye,
Sleepy little baby,
  A-ha-hum!
—Cheyenne Lullaby

SLEEP, sleep, sleep!
  Little beetles in the grass
On their mothers' backs are sleeping;
So on my back, baby mine,
Sleep, sleep, sleep!
—Hopi Lullaby

IHI! Ihi! Ihi!
  Thy father is Eagle-go-high!
Chief of the tribe is he!
Thy mother's Storm-Dancer, Storm-Dancer,
Daughter of Winds is she!
—Nootka Lullaby

Song is the natural expression of the American Indian. Feeling deeply the rhythm of nature and the beauty about him, he makes songs and dances of the sun and the wind, the rain, and of all growing things.

BUTTERFLIES, butterflies,
Fly away to the flowers,
Fly, blue wing,
Fly, yellow wing,
Fly away to the flowers!

"Polaina, polaina," *Pueblo Song*

PRETTY, see the cloud appear!
Pretty, see the rain draw near!
Who spoke?
'Twas the little ear of corn
High up on the cornstalk borne.
Corn ear, what have you to say?
"I'm so thirsty, thirsty, Rain!
Give me a drink now! Come my way!"

"Elu honkwa lonan iyane," *Zuni Song*

American Rhymes

QUAKER, Quaker, how is thee?
  Very well, I thank thee.
How's thy neighbor next to thee?
  I don't know but I'll go see! *
          —Philadelphia and Eastern States

I'M GOING to Lady Washington's,
    To get a cup of tea,
And five loaves of gingerbread,
    So don't you follow me!
          —Eastern United States

*As children sit in a ring, playing this game, one child asks his neighbor the question, wiggling his right hand. Each child does this in turn. Then each wiggles left hand, both hands, right foot, left foot, both feet, and, finally, both hands and feet together.

HERE'S the church
    And here's the steeple;
Open the door
And see all the people! *

CINDERELLA dressed in green
    Went upstairs to eat ice-cream;
Cinderella dressed in lace
Went upstairs to powder her face.
                    —*Pennsylvania*

*Children lock hands, fingers down, thumbs close together to represent the church door, and forefingers up and joined for the spire. With "Open the door!" they open their hands, fingers still locked, and wiggle the fingers to represent people.

WAKE up, Jacob—
   Day's a-breakin'
Peas in the pot
And hoecakes a-bakin'!
                    —Texas

RING around a rosy
      Sit upon a posy
All the children in our town
Sing for Uncle Josy.

                    —Maryland

TING-A-LING-LING, the scissors' grinder
   Lost his wife and couldn't find her.
                    —Maryland

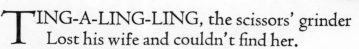

ENGINE, engine number nine
     Running along the Chicago line;
Engine, engine number nine
When she's polished, she will shine.

—*Middle West*

ALL the cats consulted;
     What was it about?
How to catch a little mouse
Running in and out.

—*Maryland*

THERE was a farmer had a dog
     Bingo was his name
   B-i-n-g-o
   B-i-n-g-o
Bingo was his name.

—*Maryland*

STAR light, star bright,
Very first star I've seen tonight;
I wish you may, I wish you might
Give me the wish I wish tonight.

MANY, many stars are in the skies
As old, as old as Adam;
Fall upon your knees
And kiss whom you please—
Your humble servant, Madam!

—Georgia

THE ROSE is red, the violet's blue,
Sugar's sweet and so are you.
If you love me as I love you,
No knife can cut our love in two.
My love for you will never fail
As long as pussy has her tail.

JINGLE BELLS, Jingle bells,
 Jingle all the way!
O what fun it is to ride
In a one-horse open sleigh!

IT SNOWS and it blows, and it cuts off my nose,
 So pray, little girl, let me in;
I'll light my pipe and warm my toes,
And then I'll be gone again!*

OVER the river and through the woods
 To Grandmother's house we go!
The horse knows the way to carry the sleigh
Through the drifts and blinding snow.

—*Lydia Maria Child*

*In this game, a child outside a circle of children pleads to come in. Being admitted, he performs the designated actions, lights his pipe and warms his toes. Then he suddenly tries to get out of the ring, throwing himself against the children's clasped hands.

ICE-COLD lemonade
Made in the shade;
Stirred with a spade
By an old maid.

PINNY, pinny, poppy show!
Give me a pin and I'll let you know!
A pin to see the poppet show!

MARY had a little lamb,
Its fleece was white as snow;
And everywhere that Mary went,
The lamb was sure to go.
It followed her to school one day,
Which was against the rule;
It made the children laugh and play,
To see a lamb in school.*

*Mary's little lamb was a real lamb who followed Mary Sawyer to the Redstone School House in Massachusetts, about 1820.
This American folk song has gathered verses through the years. Mrs. Sarah J. Hale and John Roulstone both claim its authorship.

A-TISKET, A-tasket,
A green and yellow basket,
I wrote a letter to my love,
And on the way I dropped it.
I dropped it, I dropped it!
A little boy picked it up
And put it in his pocket,
Pocket, pocket!*

WE'VE come to see Miss Jenny Jones.
And how is she today?
Miss Jenny Jones is washing,
You can't see her today.

*Children in a circle sing this song as one child runs around the circle and drops a handkerchief behind a second child who chases him as he tries to reach the vacant place. If caught, he takes the kerchief for the next game.

GO TO SLEEPY, little baby;
When you awake
I'll give you ginger cake,
And a whole lot of little horses:
One will be red,
One will be blue,
One will be the color of your mammy's shoe!

—Georgia

BABY BYE, here's a fly,
Let us watch him, you and I.
How he crawls on the walls,
Yet he never falls.
If you and I had six such legs
We could surely walk on eggs.
There he goes on his toes,
Tickling baby's nose.

BYE-O! Bye-O!
Baby's in the cradle sleeping.
Tip-toe, tip-toe,
Soft and low, like pussy creeping,
Bye-O, Bye-O!

—Georgia

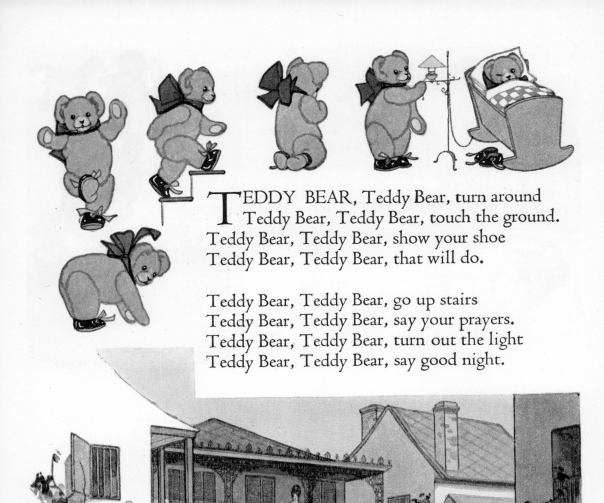

TEDDY BEAR, Teddy Bear, turn around
Teddy Bear, Teddy Bear, touch the ground.
Teddy Bear, Teddy Bear, show your shoe
Teddy Bear, Teddy Bear, that will do.

Teddy Bear, Teddy Bear, go up stairs
Teddy Bear, Teddy Bear, say your prayers.
Teddy Bear, Teddy Bear, turn out the light
Teddy Bear, Teddy Bear, say good night.

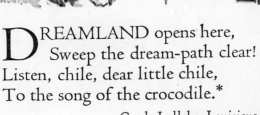

DREAMLAND opens here,
Sweep the dream-path clear!
Listen, chile, dear little chile,
To the song of the crocodile.*
　　　　　—Creole Lullaby, Louisiana

*Creoles, the French and Spanish settlers of Louisiana, left many songs and lullabies. Important contributions to the folk literature of the South, these songs reflect life on the winding bayous and the whisper of wind through trees hung with Spanish moss.

HURRY up, engine, and hurry up, train,
    Missie's going to ride on the road again,
Swift as lightning and smooth as glass—
Take off your hat when the train goes past.

               —*Southern States*

WHEN I go a-courting,
    I'll go on the train.
When I go to marry,
I'll marry Liza Jane!

               —*Southern States*

GET out of the way
for old Dan Tucker,
He's come too late to get his supper.
Supper's over and breakfast's cooking,
Old Dan Tucker's standing looking.
—*North Carolina*

I'M Captain Jinks of the Horse Marines,
I feed my horse on corn and beans,
Although it's quite beyond the means
Of a Captain in the army.

CHARLEY, barley, buck and rye,
What's the way the Frenchmen fly?
Some fly east and some fly west
And some fly over the cuckoo's nest!

—Maine

I'M a peddler, I'm a peddler,
I'm a peddler from Connecticut,
I'm a peddler, I'm a peddler,
And don't you want to buy?*

*This rhyme keeps alive the memory of the Connecticut peddlers so welcomed by lonely farm wives when they visited scattered farms in New England, and pioneer territory west to the Ohio, carrying an assortment of clocks, thread, buttons, beads, and seeds.

O MY dame had a lame tame crane;
   And my dame had a lame tame crane;
Pray, gentle Jane, let my dame's lame tame crane
Drink and come back home again!

—Maryland

WHAT'S your name? Puddin' Tame.
      Where do you live? Up Red Lane.
What's your number?
Twenty-two Cumber.

—Maryland

THE man who has plenty of good peanuts
   And giveth his neighbor none,
He shan't have any of my peanuts
When his peanuts are gone.*

—New England

*An old Yankee tune sung in New England ports in the days when New England was distinguished for baked beans, codfish, fishing fleets, and great trading ships that sailed to China and India and on all the Seven Seas.

HERE we sail so fast and free
　　And the frog in the sea
He can't catch me!
　　He, he, he!
　　He, he, he!
The frog in the sea, he can't catch me!
　　　　　　　　　　　　—*Maryland*

HERE come three jolly, jolly sailor boys
　　Just lately come for shore;
They spend their time in a merry, merry way
Just as they did before!*
　　　　　　　　　　　　—*Maryland*

*This rhyme survives from the days when great white-winged clipper ships, the fastest boats on the seas, sailing around Cape Horn and off to China and India, thronged New England's ports, dumping jolly sailors ashore. See Index: *Old Stormalong.*

WHEN Uncle Henry was a little tiny boy
A-sittin' on his daddy's knee,
He said: "If I ever grow up to be a man,
A steamboat man I want to be!"

—*Mississippi Boatman's Song*

THE boatman he's a lucky man!
No one can do as the boatman can;
The boatmen dance and the boatmen sing,
The boatman is up to everything!
Hi-O, away we go,
Floating down the river on the O-hi-O!*

—*Ohio River Boatman's Song*

*A song of the gay and adventurous young boatmen who manned flatboats on the Ohio and Mississippi rivers in the early 19th Century. Steamboats replaced flatboats about 1830, and beautiful floating palaces plied the rivers till after the Civil War.

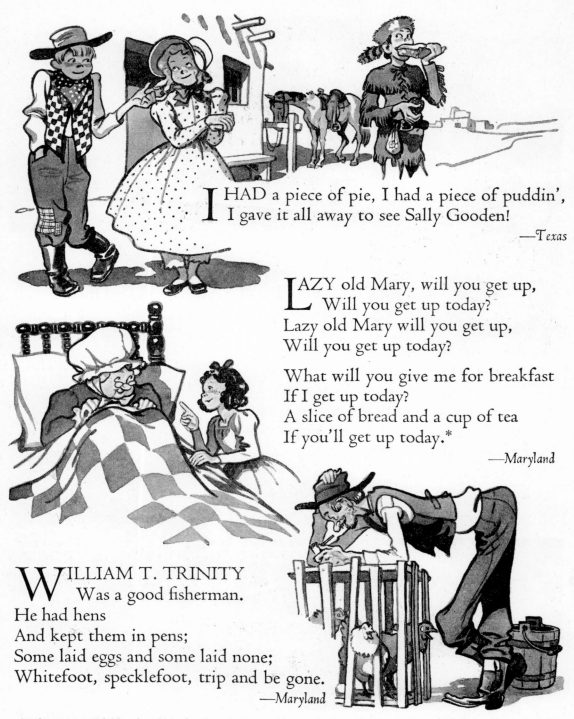

I HAD a piece of pie, I had a piece of puddin',
I gave it all away to see Sally Gooden!

—Texas

LAZY old Mary, will you get up,
Will you get up today?
Lazy old Mary will you get up,
Will you get up today?

What will you give me for breakfast
If I get up today?
A slice of bread and a cup of tea
If you'll get up today.*

—Maryland

WILLIAM T. TRINITY
Was a good fisherman.
He had hens
And kept them in pens;
Some laid eggs and some laid none;
Whitefoot, specklefoot, trip and be gone.

—Maryland

*In this game, one child, as lazy Mary, kneels with closed eyes in the center of a ring of children while another sings: "Will you get up?" Mary refuses through many verses until she is offered a nice young man for breakfast. Then she gets up.

98

OVER the hill to feed my sheep
  Over the hill to Charley
Over the hill to feed my sheep
On buckwheat cakes and barley.*

—*Kentucky Mountains*

CHARLEY'S neat and Charley's sweet;
  Charley he's a dandy;
Every time he goes to town,
He gets his girl some candy.*

—*Kentucky Mountains*

ONE, two, three, four;
  Jennie at the cottage door;
Five, six, seven, eight;
Eating cherries off a plate.

—*Maryland*

*The name Charley shows Kentucky mountaineers kept alive their memory of Bonny Prince Charley. Oppressed in Scotland for their love of Stuart pretenders to the English throne, they came to Kentucky and Tennessee in the 18th Cent. (See pp. 34, 115).

JOHN BROWN had a little Indian,
  One little Indian boy.
One little, two little, three little Indians,
Four little, five little, six little Indians,
Seven little, eight little, nine little Indians,
Ten little Indian boys!

O I'M a jolly old cowboy,
  Just off the Texas Plains;
My trade is cinching saddles,
And pulling bridle reins.
It's I can throw the lasso
With the greatest ease,
And mount my bronco pony,
And ride him when I please!*
—*Texas Cowboy Song*

*In lonely canyons of the Rocky Mountains and cattle ranches of the West, cowboys, having little to entertain them, composed many songs of the trail which they sang as they rode on horseback or sat around campfires at night. See Index: *Pecos Bill.*

FATHER and I went down to camp
Along with Captain Gooding,
And there we saw the men and boys
As thick as hasty pudding.

Yankee Doodle, keep it up
Yankee Doodle dandy,
Mind the music and the step
And with the girls be handy!

But I can't tell you half I saw,
They kept up such a smother;
I took my hat off, made a bow,
And scampered home to mother.

Amused at the awkward-looking American recruits who poured into camp in 1775, the British made up the words and tune for Yankee Doodle; but the Americans, unabashed, took over the song, added their own words and sang it with gusto.

THE farmer in the dell
The farmer in the dell
Heigho, the dairy-oh,
The farmer in the dell.

The farmer takes a wife
The farmer takes a wife
Heigho, the dairy-oh,
The farmer takes a wife.

The wife takes a child
The wife takes a child
Heigho, the dairy-oh,
The wife takes a child.

The child takes a nurse
The child takes a nurse
Heigho, the dairy-oh,
The child takes a nurse.

The nurse takes a cat
The nurse takes a cat
Heigho, the dairy-oh,
The nurse takes a cat.

The cat takes a rat
The cat takes a rat
Heigho, the dairy-oh,
The cat takes a rat.

The rat takes the cheese
The rat takes the cheese
Heigho, the dairy-oh,
The rat takes the cheese.

The cheese stands alone
The cheese stands alone
Heigho, the dairy-oh,
The cheese stands alone!

In this game, a child as the farmer stands in a circle of children while all sing. He chooses one child to stand in the ring. This child chooses another who in turn chooses another. The last child chosen is the cheese and must begin the song again as the farmer.

GO ASK your mother for fifty cents
    To see the elephant jump the fence,
He jumped so high, he touched the sky
And never came down till the Fourth of July!

I WENT to the Animal Fair,
    The birds and the beasts were there,
And the old baboon,
By the light of the moon,
Was combing his auburn hair.

JUMBO* was an elephant
  As large as all creation,
He sailed across the ocean
To join the Yankee nation.

Jumbo, Lumbo, Slombo, Jum,
Bound to see old Jumbo.

He jars the ground as he turns around,
Jumbo, elephant Jumbo;
Biggest animal in this world,
Barnum's elephant Jumbo!

He swallows peanuts by the ton.
I tell you he's a snorter!
'Lasses, cake and gingerbread,
And gone on soda water!

He lifts his trunk and growls a growl—
It's like a clap of thunder.
When it comes, the people stare,
And gaze around in wonder!
                    —Kentucky

*Jumbo, the big elephant brought by Barnum from England, was a great favorite with London children. Jumbo objected to leaving
England, sat down in a London street, and would not move until dragged in a cage by twenty horses. See Vol. VIII, page 143.

A GOAT one day was feeling fine,
He ate ten shirts from off the line!
—*American Negro*

I HAD a little dog and his name was True,
He showed me a hole in the crack of the fence
Where the pig went through!
—*American Negro*

I HAD a little mule and his name was Jack,
I rode him on his tail to save his back.
This little mule he kicked so high,
I thought that I had touched the sky!
—*American Negro*

O F all the beasts that roam the woods,
I'd rather be a squirrel,
Curl my tail upon my back,
And travel all over the world!
—*American Negro*

The American Negro has added much to the folk literature of our country. With his love of laughter and rhythm, he has given us lively dances and songs, and, in addition to these, the beautiful Negro spirituals.

ALL AROUND the cobbler's bench
The monkey chased the weasel!
The monkey thought 'twas all in fun;
Pop! goes the weasel!

—*American Rural Song*

THERE was an old pig, she lived in a sty,
And three little piggies had she.
She waddled around saying, Onk, Onk, Onk!
While the little ones said, Wee, Wee!

I SAW a crow a-flying low
And a cat a-spinning tow;
Kitty alone a-lee,
Rock-a-mary-a-ree!

—*Kentucky Mountains*

WHERE, O where has my little dog gone,
O where and O where can he be,
With his hair cut short and his tail cut long,
O where and O where can he be?*

—*German-American*

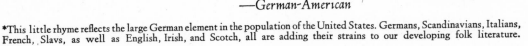

*This little rhyme reflects the large German element in the population of the United States. Germans, Scandinavians, Italians, French, Slavs, as well as English, Irish, and Scotch, all are adding their strains to our developing folk literature.

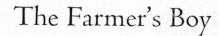

The Farmer's Boy

WHEN I was a farmer, a farmer's boy,
I used to keep my master's horses,
With a gee-wo here, and a gee-wo there,
Here a gee, and there a gee,
And everywhere a gee-wo.

When I was a farmer, a farmer's boy,
I used to keep my master's cows,
With a moo-moo here,
and a moo-moo there,
Here a moo, and there a moo,
And everywhere a moo-moo.

When I was a farmer, a farmer's boy,
I used to keep my master's chickens,
With a cluck-cluck here,
and a cluck-cluck there,
Here a cluck, and there a cluck,
And everywhere a cluck-cluck!

When I was a farmer, a farmer's boy,
I used to keep my master's dogs,
With a bow-wow here,
and a bow-wow there,
Here a bow, and there a wow,
And everywhere a bow-wow!

When I was a farmer, a farmer's boy,
I used to keep my master's ducks,
With a quack-quack here,
        and a quack-quack there,
Here a quack, and there a quack,
And everywhere a quack-quack!

When I was a farmer, a farmer's boy,
I used to keep my master's turkeys,
With a gobble-gobble here,
        and a gobble-gobble there,
Here a gobble, there a gobble,
Everywhere a gobble-gobble!

When I was a farmer, a farmer's boy,
I used to keep my master's lambs,
With a baa-baa here,
        and a baa-baa there,
Here a baa, and there a baa,
And everywhere a baa-baa!

When I was a farmer, a farmer's boy,
I used to keep my master's pigs,
With a grunt-grunt here,
        and a grunt-grunt there,
Here a grunt, and there a grunt,
And everywhere a grunt-grunt!

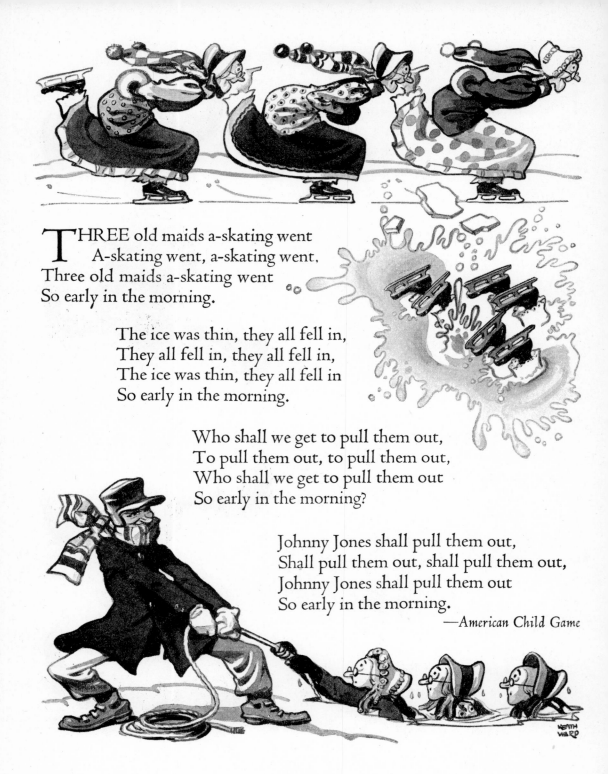

THREE old maids a-skating went
A-skating went, a-skating went.
Three old maids a-skating went
So early in the morning.

The ice was thin, they all fell in,
They all fell in, they all fell in,
The ice was thin, they all fell in
So early in the morning.

Who shall we get to pull them out,
To pull them out, to pull them out,
Who shall we get to pull them out
So early in the morning?

Johnny Jones shall pull them out,
Shall pull them out, shall pull them out,
Johnny Jones shall pull them out
So early in the morning.

—*American Child Game*

Froggie Goes a-Courting*

FROGGIE, a-courting he did ride,
   Sword and pistol by his side.
He rode up to Miss Mouse's door
Where he had never been before.
He took Miss Mouse upon his knee,
Says,"Miss Mouse will you marry me?"
"Without my Uncle Rat's consent
I would not marry the President!"
Then Uncle Rat went down to town
To buy his niece a wedding gown.
O where will the wedding supper be?
A way down yonder in the hollow tree.
O what will the wedding supper be?
Three green beans and a black-eyed pea!
The first came in was a little moth;
He spread out the tablecloth;
The next came in was a bumble-bee
With his fiddle on his knee.
The next came in was a nimble flea
To dance a jig with the bumble-bee.

—*Kentucky Mountains*

Froggie Goes a-Courting, a ballad of the Tennessee and Kentucky Mountains, reminiscent of old English folk songs, has its counterpart in many countries. *Reen-Reen-Reeny* (Vol. II, p. 37) is a Spanish-American version found in Colombia.

Old Noah

OLD Noah did build himself an ark;
  He built one out of hickory bark;
There's one wide river to cross.

The animals went in two by two,
The elephant and the kangaroo;
There's one wide river to cross.

The animals went in three by three,
The big baboon and the chimpanzee;
There's one wide river to cross.

The animals went in four by four,
The hippopotamus blocked the door;
There's one wide river to cross!

—*New England Song*

New England children entertained themselves on the way to Sunday
School by making up countless verses for this ballad of the Biblical Noah.

Turkey in the Straw

AS I came down the new-cut road,
   Met Mr. Bullfrog, met Miss Toad,
And every time Miss Toad would sing,
Old Bullfrog cut a pigeon-wing!

Turkey in the hay, Turkey in the straw,
Roll 'em up and twist 'em up
A high tuck-a-haw,
And hit 'em up a tune
Called Turkey in the Straw!

I came to the river and I couldn't get across
Paid five dollars for an old blind hoss
Wouldn't go ahead, nor he wouldn't stand still
So he went up and down like an old sawmill

—*American Rural Song*

When young people gathered together for barn dances in the South and Middle West,
fiddlers always struck up the tune, *Turkey in the Straw*, and the dancers danced a reel.

The Barnyard

I HAD a cat and the cat pleased me,
 I fed my cat under yonder tree,
And my little cat went fiddle-dee-dee.

I had a hen and the hen pleased me,
I fed my hen under yonder tree,
And my little hen went cluck-cluck-cluck,
And the cat went fiddle-dee-dee.

I had a duck and the duck pleased me,
I fed my duck under yonder tree,
And my little duck went quack-quack-quack,
And my little hen went cluck-cluck-cluck,
And the cat went fiddle-dee-dee.

I had a pig and the pig pleased me,
I fed my pig under yonder tree,
And my little pig went grunt-grunt-grunt,
And my little duck went quack-quack-quack,
And my little hen went cluck-cluck-cluck,
And the cat went fiddle-dee-dee.

I had a cow and the cow pleased me,
I fed my cow under yonder tree,
And my little cow went moo-moo-moo,
And my little pig went grunt-grunt-grunt,
And my little duck went quack-quack-quack,
And my little hen went cluck-cluck-cluck,
And the cat went fiddle-dee-dee.

I had a dog and the dog pleased me,
I fed my dog under yonder tree,
And my little dog went bow-wow-wow,
And my little cow went moo-moo-moo,
And my little pig went grunt-grunt-grunt,
And my little duck went quack-quack-quack,
And my little hen went cluck-cluck-cluck,
And the cat went fiddle-dee-dee.

I had a baby and the baby pleased me,
I fed my baby under yonder tree,
And my little baby went ma-ma-ma,
And my little dog went bow-wow-wow,
And my little cow went moo-moo-moo,
And my little pig went grunt-grunt-grunt,
And my little duck went quack-quack-quack,
And my little hen went cluck-cluck-cluck,
And the cat went fiddle-dee-dee.

—Kentucky Mountain Song

Shut up in the mountains of Kentucky and Tennessee away from the world, the mountaineers, driven from Scotland for devotion to the Stuarts, formed a folk literature all their own based on their old Scotch ballads and songs. See page 99.

Pennsylvania Dutch Rhymes

RIDE, ride a horsey,
Everybody's gone away.
Bring Dawdy home a pretzel
When you come home today!

Trot, trot, jolt!
The farmer has a colt.
The colt he runs away,
The farmer falls, hooray!
Bump!   Goes the farmer!

So ride, so ride the children,
When they still are wee;
When they're older then of course
They will ride upon a horse,
Ride to lands beyond the seas,
Where pretty maidens grow on trees!
If I had thought of that before
I'd have brought one to your door!

—Reite, reite, Gäuli

Among the many race groups melting into the American nation, none has a richer nursery lore than the Pennsylvania Dutch who developed a distinct dialect in America. *Hei, Jim Along Josey* is an amusing mixture of Pennsylvania Dutch and English.

BYE-LO, Bubbeli, sleep,
  Your dawdy guards the sheep,
Your mommy tends the little red cow
And she'll be coming home soon now.

  —*Hei-yo Bubbeli schlof*

HEI, Jim along Josey,
  Der Bullfrog in der Spring!
The water was so cold,
He could not swim.

I STAND in the pulpit and preach;
  The animals I must teach.
My rooster and my hen,
My sermon I begin.
My cow and my calf
My sermon is half.
My cat and my mouse
You can all leave the house!

  —*Da stehn ich uf der Kanzel*

Lullabies

SWEET AND LOW

SWEET and low, sweet and low,
    Wind of the western sea,
Low, low, breathe and blow,
    Wind of the western sea,
Over the rolling waters go,
    Come from the dying moon, and blow,
Blow him again to me;
    While my little one, while my pretty one, sleeps.

Sleep and rest, sleep and rest,
    Father will come to thee soon;
Rest, rest, on mother's breast,
    Father will come to thee soon.
Father will come to his babe in the nest,
    Silver sails all out of the west
Under the silver moon.
    Sleep, my little one, sleep, my pretty one, sleep.

—*Alfred Tennyson*

MATILDA BREVER

There is beautiful music for this lullaby by Tennyson and also for many nursery rhymes. In most countries rhymes are sung to babies rather than spoken as in England and America. Interest is first awakened in them by music.

THE SLEEPY SONG*

As soon as the fire burns red and low
    And the house upstairs is still,
She sings me a queer little sleepy song
    Of sheep that go over the hill.

The good little sheep run quick and soft;
    Their colors are gray and white;
They follow their leader, nose and tail,
    For they must be home by night.

And one slips over, and one comes next,
    And one runs after behind;
The gray one's nose at the white one's tail,
    The top of the hill they find.

And when they get to the top of the hill,
    They quietly slip away;
But one runs over and one comes next—
    Their colors are white and gray.

And one slips over and one comes next,
    The good little, gray little sheep!
I watch how the fire burns red and low,
    And she says that I fall asleep.

        —*Josephine Daskam Bacon*

*From "*Poems*" by Josephine Daskam Bacon; copyright, 1903, by Charles Scribner's Sons, Publishers.

119

German Nursery Rhymes

A B, C,
   Kitty's in the snow I see!
When she comes back home again
She has little white boots then!
O Jimminy! O Jo!

A, B, C,
Kitty climbs a tree!
She licks her little cold, cold feet,
She cleans her booties off so neat,
And goes no more out in the snow!
O Jimminy! O Jo!

   —A, B, C, *die Katz'lief in den Schnee*

LITTLE Liese comes a-running.
Who'll buy my little calf?
How much do you want for him?
A penny and a half!

A penny and a half's too much!
A broomstick's all I'll pay!
Then take him for a broomstick;
I don't want him anyway!

—*Die Liese kommt gelaufen*

WOULD you like to see goats dance on stilts?
Then to Crazy-town you must go.
The cow wears slippers on her feet,
And everyone laughs, Ho-ho!

The ducks laugh, quack, quack, quack!
The farm-boy laughs till he cries;
And over there the dog, the dog,
The dog makes Big Round Eyes!

—*Willst du Ziegen auf Stelzen tanzen sehn*

THE cuckoo and the donkey
Each boasted one fine day,
That he could sing the sweetest song
To greet the lovely May.

Said Cuckoo: "I sing sweetly!"
And straight he did begin.
"But I can sing still better!"
The donkey he joined in!

Their song was sweet and lovely
And quite without a flaw;
For those two sang together,—
"Cuckoo! Cuckoo! Ee-aw!"

—*Der Kuckuck und der Esel*

SUM-M, SUM-M, SUM-M!
Little bee come, hum-m!
We won't hurt you, we'll be good!
Fly away to field and wood!
Sum-m, Sum-m, Sum-m!
Little bee, come, hum-m!

—"Summ, summ, summ," *Bienchen summ herum*

HOP, my horsey, leap and spring,
And a little song I'll sing.
Over stick and stone you go,
Never tired and never slow.
Hop, hop, hop, hop!
Gallop-a-trot, hop-hop!

See how green's the meadow grass
Flowers are springing as we pass,
Birds are singing O heigho,
All along the way we go.
Hop, hop, hop, hop!
Gallop-a-trot, hop-hop!

There's our house now through the trees
Hurry horsey if you please—
Mother's waiting, mother dear!
Whoa, my horsey, now stop here!
Hop, hop, hop, hop!
Gallop-a-trot, hop-hop!
—*Hopp, mein Pferdchen*—
du sollst springen

HOLLING

French Nursery Rhymes

KING Dagobert once wore
His breeches turned hindside before.
Said Eloi, the friar:
"Oh, my King and Sire,
Those breeches on you,
Are all wrongside to!"
The King said: "You don't say!
Then I'll turn them the other way!"*

—Le bon roi Dagobert

CATHERINE, my dearie,
Wake up now I pray.
Look out of your window,
Here's May and a bouquet!

—Catherine, ma mie

THERE was an old dame called Tartine
Had a house made of butter and cream;
Its walls were of flour, it is said,
And its floors were of gingerbread!

Her bed she did make
Of white frosted cake;
And her pillow at night
Was a biscuit so light!

—Il était une Dame Tartine

*King Dagobert (7th Cent.) was the only really active ruler among the "Do-Nothing Kings" of France who were finally deposed by Pepin, Mayor of the Palace and father of Charlemagne. King Dagobert's throne is still shown at St. Denis.

AT the wedding of Miss Jenny Wren,
   The bridegroom was so wee.
"Go ask the wedding guests to come
To the wedding feast," said he.

O come to the wedding, birdies all
And each a present bring!
"I'll come," said the cock.   "I'll come, come, come!
"And before the feast, I'll sing!"

"I'll come! I'll come!" said the big black crow,
"And bring the pair some meat!"
"I'll come, too," said the nightingale,
"I'll sing 'Tweet-tweet! Tweet-tweet!'"

"I'll bring wood," the woodpecker said,
"For Jenny and her little spouse!"
"And I'll come, too," the swallow said,
"I'll twitter on top of the house!"

At the wedding of Miss Jenny Wren,
The bridegroom was so wee,
But one and all the birdies came
That wedding for to see.

                    —*Les Noces du Roitelet*

The *Wedding of Jenny Wren* is the subject of rhymes
and tales in many countries. See Vol. II, page 212.

Dutch Nursery Rhymes

THERE was a little man and his name was Gice
He built himself a little house right on the ice.
Then he wished he had a hen.
Chip-chip is my hen,
Evenings in the little cage,
Mornings in the pen.

Then he wished he had a sheep.
Trip-treep is my sheep,
Chip-chip is my hen,
Evenings in the little cage,
Mornings in the pen.

Then he wished he had a cow.
Nonny-gow is my cow,
Trip-treep is my sheep,
Chip-chip is my hen,
Evenings in the little cage,
Mornings in the pen.

Then he wished he had a calf.
Duck-dalf is my calf,
Nonny-gow is my cow,
Trip-treep is my sheep,
Chip-chip is my hen,
Evenings in the little cage,
Mornings in the pen.

—*Daar was eens een mannetje dat heette Gijs*

126

THERE were three duckies in a brookie
    One called Bookie,
    One called Gookie,
And one called Klip-Klap-Keppelookie.
    Klip-Klap-Keppelookie found a cookie
    But he would not give it to Bookie.
So Bookie took a stone and peg!
Hit Klip-Klap-Keppelookie in the leg!
    "For shame, Bookie,"
    Then said Gookie,
"To take a stone and peg!
    Hit Klip-Klap-Keppelookie in the leg!"
      —Er waren drie eendjes in een pontje

HERE is the key to
    Bibbley-babbley-town.
In Bibbley-babbley-town
Stands a Bibbley-babbley house;
In that Bibbley-babbley house
Live the Bibbley-babbley people;
And the Bibbley-babbley people
Have some Bibbley-babbley children;
And the Bibbley-babbley children
Eat their Bibbley-babbley sup
With a Bibbley-babbley spoon
From a Bibbley-babbley cup!   *—Hier is de sleutel*

Czechoslovakian Rhymes

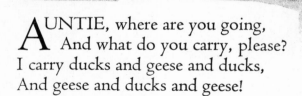

AUNTIE, where are you going,
  And what do you carry, please?
I carry ducks and geese and ducks,
And geese and ducks and geese!

I'M a butcher and you're a butcher,
  To market to buy a cow we'll go,
You'll pay the money, I'll do the talking,
With pretty maids all in a row!

KNITTING still, knitting still,
  Always knitting with a will.
Red, green, blue; red, green, blue—
I'll knit a little coat for you!

ANNIE goes to the cabbage field;
  She picks green leaves in the cabbage field
To feed her rabbits fine.
Johnny sees her, ha–ha–ha,
Says: "I'll catch you, tra–la–la."
"Nay," says she, "Now go away,
I'll not dance with you today!"
                    —Sla Nanynka do zeli

HOW strong, how strong a bridge have you?
    Ha–ya, ha–ya, ha–yo!
Over hills and valleys
    To the greenwoods we will go!
But you must pay before you cross.
And how much will you pay?
A cuckoo bird I'll give you
If you let me pass today!

Canadian Songs

ROLL it, bowl it, roll it,
  Set the ball a-rolling;
Round and round and round and round,
Roly, poly bowling.

—*En roulant ma boule*

O IF my top would only spin
  A monk's gown I would give to him.
Dance my top, go dancing.
You do not care for dancing?
You do not care how my grain is ground!
You do not care how my mill goes round!

—*Ah! si mon moine voulait danser!*

MATILDA BREUER

The songs on this page and the first on p. 131, are French-Canadian; the last on 131, is Eskimo. All have been sung at folk festivals in Quebec, where people gather, not only from the Arctic North but from all Canada's vast, diversified provinces.

THERE was an old, old Indian,
All painted and all black,
Weech-Ka!

He had an old, old blanket,
And his tobacco sack,
Weech-Ka!

—C'était un vieux sauvage

I-YAY! I-yay! I-yay!
Happy the dark winter day!
Then come friends from afar
Happy, how happy we are.
Tat-a-tat-tat! Drums beat like that.
Friends and our villagers dance away!
Yay-yay, we sing, yay-yay-yay-yay!
Happy, how happy, the dark winter day!

—Eskimo

Russian Rhymes

DON'T run away my kitty,
In the carriage you must sit;
So stay there with my dollies
And ride around a bit!"

The little girl begged nicely
But Kitty ran away;
He said, "I'm very hungry,
I'll chase the mice today!"

"I'm going in to dinner!"
He jumped and off he ran—
"And after I have eaten,
Then catch me if you can!"

SNAIL, snail
Shakety shake
Put out your horns
And I'll give you some cake!

HARK, the Christmas bells are ringing
  And the children all are singing;
Dancing round the Christmas tree,
All as happy as can be!
See the candles shining bright,
Shining bright as stars of light,
And the goodies there to eat,
Little cakes and apples sweet!
All the pretty presents see
Lying there around the tree!

LITTLE bells, pretty flowers of the steppes,
  Turning your faces my way.
Why do you droop your heads
On such a bright May day?

As you shake your heads in the grasses,
What do you whisper and say?

—Колокольчики

133

The Boy Who Made Hay

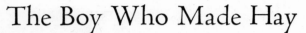

THE boy goes to the field and takes
    His scythe.

And what are you going to do with the scythe?
    Cut the grass.

And what are you going to do with the grass?
    Make it into hay.

And what are you going to do with the hay?
    Feed it to the cow.

And what are you going to do with the cow?
    Milk her.

And what are you going to do with the milk?
    Give it to the baby.

And what are you going to do with the baby?
Hug him and squeeze him and hug him and squeeze him!

    "Haa vil du?" *a Norse Nursery Rhyme*

Mary Milks the Cow

TICK-tock, five o'clock!   Mary milks the cow;
Mary milks as fast as she can, as fast as she can, can, can.

Tick-tock, six o'clock!   Mary pours the milk;
Mary pours the milk in the pan, the milk in the pan, pan, pan.

Tick-tock, seven o'clock!   The milk is in the cart;
And horsey draws the cart along, clopperty, clopperty, clop!

Tick-tock, eight o'clock! Baby drinks his milk;
Baby drinks it every drop, drinks it every drop.
"Klokken fem melker Mari," *a Norse Nursery Rhyme*

Hungarian Rhymes*

I SHOULD like to plough;
With six big oxen plough,
If my sweetheart, she
Would guide the plough for me!

—*Szeretnek szantani*

ROUND is my bun, yum, yum!
My pocket's too small
for my bun!
Break it in two! Will that do?
It fits! It fits! Hurrah for you!

—*Kerekes a zsemlye*

*These rhymes were gathered in Hungary, by Miska Petersham.

136

A Roumanian Lullaby

SLEEP, my baby, sleep an hour,
  You're my little gillyflower!
Mother rocks you; mother's near!
She will wash you baby dear,
Wash you clean in water clear,
Keep the sunshine from you here!
Sleep, my baby, sleep an hour,
Grow up like the gillyflower!

MARIEL WILHOITE

Over in the Meadow

OLIVE A. WADSWORTH

Over in the meadow,
  In the sand, in the sun,
Lived an old mother-toad
  And her little toadie one.
"Wink," said the mother;
  "I wink," said the one;
So she winked and she blinked
  In the sand, in the sun.

Over in the meadow,
  Where the stream runs blue,
Lived an old mother-fish
  And her little fishes two.
"Swim," said the mother;
  "We swim," said the two;
So they swam and they leaped
  Where the stream runs blue.

Over in the meadow,
    In a hole in a tree,
Lived an old mother-bluebird
    And her little birdies three.
"Sing," said the mother;
    "We sing," said the three;
So they sang and were glad,
    In the hole in the tree.

Over in the meadow,
    In the reeds on the shore,
Lived a mother-muskrat
    And her little ratties four.
Dive," said the mother;
    "We dive," said the four;
So they dived and they burrowed
    In the reeds on the shore.

DONN P. CRANE

Over in the meadow,
 In a snug bee-hive,
Lived a mother honey-bee
 And her little bees five.
"Buzz," said the mother;
 "We buzz," said the five;
So they buzzed and they hummed
 In the snug bee-hive.

Over in the meadow,
 In a nest built of sticks,
Lived a black mother-crow
 And her little crows six.
"Caw," said the mother;
 "We caw," said the six;
So they cawed and they called
 In their nest built of sticks.

Over in the meadow,
 Where the grass is so even,
Lived a gay mother-cricket
 And her little crickets seven.
"Chirp," said the mother;
 "We chirp," said the seven;
So they chirped cheery notes
 In the grass soft and even.

Over in the meadow,
  By the old mossy gate,
Lived a brown mother-lizard
  And her little lizards eight.
"Bask," said the mother;
  "We bask," said the eight;
So they basked in the sun
  On the old mossy gate.

Over in the meadow,
  Where the quiet pools shine,
Lived a green mother-frog
  And her little froggies nine.
"Croak," said the mother,
  "We croak," said the nine;
So they croaked and they splashed
  Where the quiet pools shine.

Over in the meadow,
  In a sly little den,
Lived a gray mother-spider
  And her little spiders ten.
"Spin," said the mother,
  "We spin," said the ten;
So they spun lace webs
  In their sly little den.

Monkeys

THE funniest thing in the world, I know,
Is watchin' the monkeys in the show!
Jumpin' and runnin' and racin' roun',
'Way up the top o' the pole, then down!
First they're here, an' then they're there,
An' just almost any an' everywhere!
Screechin' and scratchin' wherever they go,
They're the funniest thing in the world, I know!
                                    —James Whitcomb Riley

From "The Funniest Thing in the World" in *Rhymes of Childhood*, by James Whitcomb Riley, copyright 1890, 1918, used by special permission of the publishers, The Bobbs-Merrill Company.

HOW doth the little busy bee
Improve each shining hour,
And gather honey all the day
From every opening flower!*
—Isaac Watts

I LOVE little pussy, her coat is so warm,
And if I don't hurt her, she'll do me no harm.
I'll sit by the fire and give her some food,
And pussy will love me because I am good.*
—Jane Taylor

BLESSINGS on thee, dog of mine.
Pretty collars make thee fine!
—Elizabeth Barrett Browning

Flush, a cocker spaniel, was devoted to Elizabeth Barrett, the poetess. During her
long illness, he lay at her feet rather than scamper about. When Robert Browning
courted Elizabeth, it was a long time before Flush would make friends with him.
*Isaac Watts (1674-1748), preacher and hymn-writer, and Jane Taylor (1783-1824) were among the first to write for children.

Rhymes of Finland

HI-YI, hi-yi, Hytola
    The dogs of Hytola bark.
My little girl, my little boy,
Hear them coming!   Hark!
           —*Hyi, hyi, Hytölään*

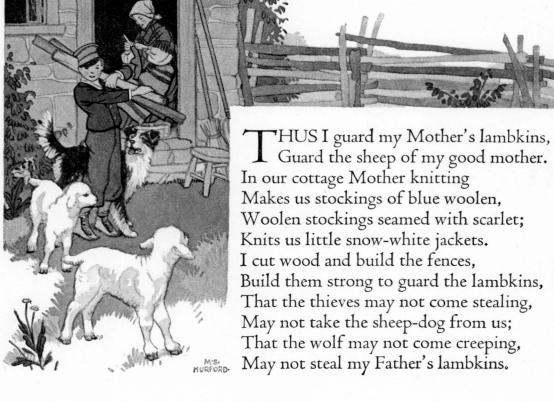

THUS I guard my Mother's lambkins,
    Guard the sheep of my good mother.
In our cottage Mother knitting
Makes us stockings of blue woolen,
Woolen stockings seamed with scarlet;
Knits us little snow-white jackets.
I cut wood and build the fences,
Build them strong to guard the lambkins,
That the thieves may not come stealing,
May not take the sheep-dog from us;
That the wolf may not come creeping,
May not steal my Father's lambkins.

COLD, son of wind and snow,
Don't nip my finger-tips!
Don't freeze my fingers, please!
Nip the water-willows!
Freeze the white birch trees!

—*Pakkanen puhurin poika*

WHEN I was a baby
Growing like a floweret,
Mother took me to the hayfield,
Took my cradle to the cornfield,
She bade the cuckoo swing me,
Called the summer bird to rock me,
So the cuckoo cuckooed gently
And the summer bird sang sweetly
While I listened full of wonder.

—*Estonian Folk Song*

African Child Rhymes

OPEN your beak, my little bird,
  Open your beak, my little bird!
Stir the porridge, do not spill it—
Mother, I will eat the millet!
Give my bird the Kafir corn—
Let us eat, for it is morn.
                    —*Central Africa, Congo*

SLEEP, sleep, my little one! The night is all wind and rain;
  The meal has been wet by the raindrops
        and bent is the sugar cane;
O Giver who gives to the people, in safety my little son keep!
My little son with the headdress, sleep, sleep, sleep!
                    —*East Africa, Abyssinia*

These rhymes were gathered by Holling C. Holling from manuscripts of African folk lore at the Field Museum, Chicago.

THE HOLLINGS

CHILD, I must sweep the hut today;
　Sisters, grind the meal I pray!
To hunt the elephants Father's gone,
On the elephant hunt the Chief has gone!
Little Cuma climbs a tree;
Watching the road he sings, sings he;
"It's far where my father's gone today,
Away, way off, away and away!"
　　　　　　　—West Africa, Cameroon

THE drums call the village to dance,
　I'm coming today to dance—
Tum, tum! Tum, tum, goes the drum!
　　　—South Africa, Rhodesia

Rhymes from Shakespeare

AS it fell upon a day
   In the merry month of May,
Beasts did leap and birds did sing,
Trees did grow and plants did spring.

IN the Springtime,
   The only pretty ring time,
When birds do sing,
Hey-ding-a-ding-ding!
Sweet lovers love the Spring.

JOG on, jog on, the footpath way,
   And merrily jump the stile, boys;
A merry heart goes all the day,
   Your sad one tires in a mile, boys.

HARK, hark!
   Bow-wow!
The watch dog's bark;
   Bow-wow!
   Hark, hark!
I hear the strains of strutting chanticleer
Cry "cock-a-diddle-dow!"

KING Stephen was a worthy peer,
   His breeches cost him but a crown,
He held them sixpence all too dear;
With that he called the tailor clown!

WHEN that I was but a little tiny boy,
   With hey-ho, the wind and the rain,
A foolish thing was but a toy,
For the rain it raineth every day!

149

TOMMY was a silly boy,
  "I can fly," he said;
He started off, but very soon,
  He tumbled on his head.

His little sister Prue was there,
  To see how he would do it;
She knew that, after all his boast,
  Full dearly Tom would rue it!
                    —*Kate Greenaway*

Kate Greenaway (1846-1901) was the first great illustrator for children. Flowers, children, prim little gardens were her delight and her simple frocks and aprons, hats and breeches set the fashion in dress both in England and America.

HIGGLEDY, piggledy! see how they run!
Hopperty, popperty! what is the fun?
Has the sun or moon tumbled into the sea?
What is the matter, now? Pray tell it me!

Higgledy, piggledy! how can I tell?
Hopperty, popperty! hark to the bell!
The rats and the mice even scamper away;
Who can say what may not happen to-day?

—*Kate Greenaway*

Although she lived in London, Kate Greenaway visited in Nottinghamshire as a girl, and she so loved the freshness and charm of
the English countryside that she pictured it delightfully in her books. See *Marigold Garden, Under the Window, Mother Goose.*

Verses by John Keats

THERE was a naughty boy,
A naughty boy was he,
He kept little fishes
In washing tubs three.

CHILD, I see thee!   Child, I spy thee!
And thy mother sweet is nigh thee!

WHERE be you going, you Devon maid?
And what have ye there in the basket?
Ye bright little fairy just fresh from the dairy,
Will ye give me some cream if I ask it?

MATILDA BREUER

Verses by Robert Burns

O Lady Mary Ann
　　Looked o'er the castle wall;
She saw three bonnie boys
　　Playing at the ball.

THE ploughman he's a bonnie lad,
　　His mind is ever true, Jo,
His garters knit below his knee,
　　His bonnet it is blue, Jo!

O RATTLIN', roarin' Willie,
　　O he hied to the fair,
An' for to sell his fiddle
　　An' buy some other ware!

MATILDA BREUER

Poems by Alfred Tennyson

WHAT does little birdie say
   In her nest at peep of day?
Let me fly, says little birdie,
Mother, let me fly away.
Birdie, rest a little longer,
Till the little wings are stronger,
So she rests a little longer,
Then she flies away.

O WELL for the fisherman's boy,
   That he shouts with his sister at play!
O well for the sailor lad,
That he sings in his boat on the bay!

DAINTY little maiden, whither would you wander?
Whither from this pretty home, the home where
mother dwells?
"Far and far away," said the dainty little maiden,
"All among the gardens, auriculas, anemones,
Roses and lilies and Canterbury-bells."

Poems by Christina Rossetti

MINNIE and Mattie
And fat little May,
Out in the country,
Spending a day.

Pinky white pigling
Squeals through his snout,
Woolly white lambkin
Frisks all about.

A WHITE hen sitting
On white eggs three:
Next, three speckled chickens
As plump as plump can be.

From *Sing Song* by Christina Rossetti. By permission of The Macmillan Company, publishers.

MIX a pancake,
  Stir a pancake,
  Pop it in the pan;
Fry the pancake,
Toss the pancake,
  Catch it if you can.

LIE a-bed,
  Sleepy head,
Shut up eyes, bo-peep;
Till day-break
Never wake:
Baby, sleep.

O SAILOR, come ashore,
  What have you brought for me?
Red coral, white coral,
  Coral from the sea.

A woman who always delighted in the simple joys of children was Christina Rossetti (English, 1830-1894), the author of *Sing Song*. She was a sister of the poet and painter, Dante Gabriel Rossetti, and often sat as a model for him while he painted.

Poems by Robert Louis Stevenson

OF speckled eggs the birdie sings
And nests among the trees;
The sailor sings of ropes and things
In ships upon the seas.

The children sing in far Japan,
The children sing in Spain;
The organ with the organ man
Is singing in the rain.

Best-loved of children's poets, Robert Louis Stevenson, born in Edinburgh, in 1850, tells in A Child's Garden of Verses of the lively world of romance he created as a child when illness kept him much in bed shut away from childish pleasures.

WHEN I was down beside the sea
A wooden spade they gave to me
To dig the sandy shore.
My holes were empty like a cup.
In every hole the sea came up,
Till it could come no more.

THE friendly cow all red and white
I love with all my heart:
She gives me cream with all her might,
To eat with apple-tart.

BRING the comb and play upon it!
Marching, here we come!
Willie cocks his highland bonnet,
Johnnie beats the drum.

159

First Adventures

MOTHER put Janie in a gocart and out they went for a walk—
Walkety, walkety, walk!
And Janie saw a little dog;
    And Janie said, "Hello!"—
    And the little dog said, "Bow-wow!"
And Mother and Janie and the gocart went walkety, walkety, walk!
And Janie saw a little cat;
    And Janie said, "Hello!"—
    And the little cat said, "Miaow!"
And Mother and Janie and the gocart went walkety, walkety, walk!
Then Janie said, "Janie walk."
And Mother stopped the gocart, and she took Janie out of the cart
and she put Janie down on the sidewalk. And Janie walked all by herself—
    Walkety, walkety, walk!
And Janie saw a little girl coming along the street.
    And Janie said, "Hello!"—
    And the little girl said, "Hello!"
And Janie went walkety, walk! Walkety, walkety, walk!

The first prose stories children enjoy are bits of their own experience; the things they see, hear, taste and smell; the joy of activity in using their bodies. Mothers and fathers can spin such stories endlessly on short simple themes.

And Janie ran up to a store and she stopped to peep in a window.

And Janie saw a little boy sitting in a barber's chair having his hair cut, snip!

And Janie said, "Hello!"—

And the scissors said, "Snip, snip, snip!"

And Janie laughed at the scissors and off she went walkety, walkety! Walkety, walkety, walk!

And Janie saw a great big man coming along the street.

And Janie ran up to the man.

And Janie said, "Hello, Daddy!"—

And the man said, "Hello, Janie!"

And Daddy picked Janie up and kissed her right on the cheek. Then Daddy set Janie down and he said hello to Mother and he took the go-cart from Mother and pushed it along himself. And Janie and Mother and Daddy all went home together, walkety, walkety, walk!

The Little Turtle*

(*A Recitation for Martha Wakefield, Three Years Old*)

THERE was a little turtle.
He lived in a box.
He swam in a puddle.
He climbed on the rocks.

He snapped at a mosquito.
He snapped at a flea.
He snapped at a minnow.
And he snapped at me.

He caught the mosquito.
He caught the flea.
He caught the minnow.
But he didn't catch me.

—Vachel Lindsay

MATILDA BREUER

Animal Crackers**

ANIMAL crackers, and cocoa to drink,
That is the finest of suppers, I think;
When I'm grown up and can have what I please
I think I shall always insist upon these.

—Christopher Morley

*From *Collected Poems* by Vachel Lindsay. By permission of The Macmillan Company, publishers.
**From *Chimneysmoke*, by Christopher Morley, copyright 1917, 1921, by Doubleday, Doran and Company, Inc.

Conversation*

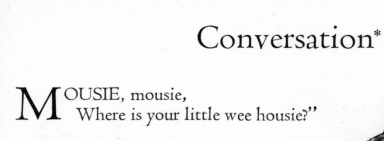

"MOUSIE, mousie,
   Where is your little wee housie?"

"Here is the door,
Under the floor,"
   Said mousie, mousie.

"Mousie, mousie,
May I come into your housie?"

"You can't get in
You have to be thin,"
   Said mousie, mousie.

"Mousie, mousie,
   Won't you come out of your housie?"

"I'm sorry to say
I'm busy all day,"
   Said mousie, mousie.
        —Rose Fyleman

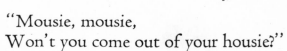

My Boat

I SAIL my boat on a tiny sea,
   Blow, wind, blow;
And some day I shall a sailor be,
   Blow, wind, blow.
        —Anonymous

MATILDA BREUER

*From *Fifty-one New Nursery Rhymes*, by Rose Fyleman, copyright 1932, by Doubleday, Doran and Company, Inc.

Building with Blocks

WHAT are you able to build with your blocks?
Castles and palaces, temples and docks.
Rain may keep raining and others go roam,
But I can be happy and building at home.

—*Robert Louis Stevenson*

O I'LL build a square with my pretty red blocks,
  And a yellow square, Sookey, for you;
I'll pile up and pile up the bright blocks of green,
  You lay on the blocks of blue.
Now see what we've made with our great big square—
  A house!   A house for Teddy Bear!

—*Olive Beaupré Miller*

Good Morning, Peter

ONCE there was a little boy named Peter and he was fast asleep in a little bed right next his mother's big bed. All of a sudden he heard:

Cock-a-doodle-doo!

That was the rooster crowing, and Peter opened his eyes.   In a few moments more, he heard:

Pit-pat, pit-pat, pit-pat,
Clopperty, clopperty, clop!

That was the milkman's horse coming up the street. And

Rattlety, rattlety, bang!

That was the milkman's wagon coming up the street. And

Clinkety, clinkety, clink!

That was the song of the bottles the milkman left at the door.

Now Peter was wide awake. So he picked up his Teddy Bear, for Teddy Bear slept every night right in the bed with Peter.

"Hello, Teddy Bear!" That is what Peter said.

But Teddy Bear said nothing.

So Peter began to rub his hand all over Teddy's fur to feel how soft it was. He rubbed and he rubbed and he rubbed. Teddy was so soft and fuzzy.

165

By and by Peter's mother opened her eyes and woke up. And Peter's mother said:

"Well, well! Good morning, Peter! Are you awake already?"

And Peter sat up in bed.

"Peter get up!" he said.

So Peter's mother got out of bed and she put on her great big bathrobe to keep her warm in the cold.

She took Peter up in her arms and carried him across to the bathroom, and Teddy Bear went along, for Peter was holding him fast.

And Peter's mother took Teddy Bear and she set him up by the washbowl to watch while Peter got dressed. Then Peter's mother sat down on a stool with Peter in her lap, and she took off Peter's nightdress. She turned on the water in the faucets and the water went

Swish, swish, spurt!   Swish, swish, sputter, splash!

The water splashed up so high it hit Teddy Bear on the nose. Peter

laughed and he squealed:

"Water hit Teddy Bear's nose!" That is what Peter squealed.

Then Peter's mother took a washcloth and she washed Peter's face and his hands. She took Peter's toothbrush down from the little hook where it hung and brush, brush, brush—she gave Peter's teeth a scrub.

And Peter's mother said:

"Teddy Bear sees Peter getting all cleaned up."

Then Peter's mother took Peter's underwear and she held it so he could

step into it. And Peter put in one leg, then he put in the other leg. And Peter put in one arm, then he put in the other arm. And Peter's mother said:

"Teddy Bear sees Peter get into his underwear."

And Peter's mother took Peter's little new suit and she held it for him. And Peter put in one leg, then he put in the other leg. And Peter put in one arm, then he put in the other arm. And Peter's mother buttoned all the buttons and Peter's mother said:

"Teddy Bear sees Peter get into his new suit."

Then Peter's mother took Peter's socks. And she put one sock on one leg and the other sock on the other leg. And Peter's mother said:

"Teddy Bear sees Peter having his socks put on."

But Peter took his shoes and what do you think he did? He put them on all by himself. And Peter's mother said:

"Good gracious, look at that! Teddy Bear sees Peter put his own shoes on!"

Then Peter's mother took a brush and comb. And slick, slick, slick, she brushed Peter's hair down smooth. And after that Peter's mother took Teddy Bear down from the washbowl and put him in Peter's arms. And Peter took Teddy Bear and ran away to play.

The Little Girl and the New Dress

ADAPTED FROM HANS CHRISTIAN ANDERSEN

ONCE there was a little girl and she had a new dress. The dress was as blue as the sky. And the little girl had a new pink hat. All the big people stood around and said:

"Oh, what a pretty new dress!" and "Oh, what a pretty new hat!"

Then the big people brought in lighted candles so they could see the little girl better. And the pussy cat came in, too, to see that pretty new dress. But the little girl said:

"Where is my little dog? He must see my new dress, too!"

Well, her little dog was off in the park playing with other dogs. So the little girl's mother said:

"Tomorrow you shall show your little dog your new dress."

Next day the little dog was scampering about the yard with the other dogs. And when the little girl went out in her new dress, her little dog came running to her in a hurry with all the other dogs chasing after him. Then the little girl smiled and said:

"They like my pretty new dress!"

OF all the girls that are so smart
    There's none like pretty Sally;
She is the darling of my heart,
    And she lives in our alley.
               —H. Carey

The Big Street in the Big City
LUCY SPRAGUE MITCHELL

SOMEWHERE there is a street. It is a long street. It is a wide street. And it runs through the middle of a big city.

On the sides of the street are sidewalks, two smooth cement sidewalks, one on each side of the street. And, on the sidewalks, walk many feet. On the sidewalks heavy feet stamp, and smaller feet tramp, and little feet skip and patter and dance.

Out on the street go all the things with wheels. They pass in a long procession. Lumbering, rumbling, whizzing, zipping, they roll down the street. First comes a clumsy motor truck lumbering along on big wheels with broad tires. Inside is a load of bricks with wisps of straw between them. Is it taking the bricks to some workmen who are building a new house? It thumps and thuds down the street. Then a taxi with a passenger whizzes by. It is black and yellow. Fast, fast it zips past, swerving and curving around the lumbering truck. It just misses the clumsy truck! Then a tremendous bus glides by with many rows of seats inside and many faces looking out of the many windows. Enormous, smoothly purring, shiny with new green and white paint.

Reprinted from *Streets*, Cooperating School Pamphlet No. 2, by permission of the Bureau of Educational Experiments, 69 Bank Street, New York, and the John Day Company.

What a racket is this coming? Pitz! pitz! pitz! What is exploding like a queer moving bunch of firecrackers? All this noise from that small thing straddled by a man in goggles? Yes, that little motorcycle is making all that racket. And look at its speed. Whew! It rushes by, dodging the truck, dodging the bus. Look it has caught up with the taxi! It has passed the whizzing taxi. And now, trotting close to the sidewalk, comes a horse with a wagon. The horse is gray with spots on his flanks and blackish mane and tail. The wagon has a milk bottle painted on its side. The driver hardly needs to hold the reins for the wise old milk horse knows his own way from house to house. He clatters by with the milk wagon and rattles down the street.

Another truck. This is full of ashes. Over the ashes is spread a big cloth. Two men sit on top. A puff of wind blows the powdery ashes out from under the cloth as the truck rolls by down the street.

More taxis, more automobiles, more wagons, more trucks! Then they all stop. Down the street a light shines red. The trucks stand still, the taxis and wagons and buses stand still. The motorcyclist spreads his legs and touches the ground with his feet. The driver says "whoa" to the gray milk horse. They all stand still on the street.

Green light! The truck driver takes off his brakes and steps on the gas. But the taxi, with a jerk, is off first. Away it whizzes. Then the big green and white bus. Pitz! pitz! pitz! The motorcyclist has his feet on the pedals again. He passes the bus; he passes the taxi; he is gone! The driver says "Go on, Dick!" and the old gray milk horse jogs off with the pretty milk wagon rattling after.

More taxis, more autos, another bus, more wagons, another motor-cycle, more trucks.

Red light! They all stop; they all stand still on the street.

Green light! Off again—first the taxis, then the bus, then the motor-cyclist who races ahead, then the trucks and then the horse—this time a bay horse that pulls a laundry wagon.

And so it happens all day—first the red light and then the green light on the long street, the wide street that runs through the middle of the big city.

The light is green!
Away they go—
Trucks and autos and wagons and bus,
   rumbling and grumbling
   or trotting and jogging
   or smoothly gliding without any fuss.

The light is red!
   Jam on the brakes—
     "Whoa!" pull on the rein!
It's changed to green.
   Step on the gas,
   "Gitty-ap!"
     They're off again!

The Green Bus*

WAIT a minute,
Green bus!
Slow down!
Stop!

I will climb
Your winding stair
And ride
On top.

Along
The busy river,
Down
The avenue,

Any day
I like to take
A trip
With you.

—*James S. Tippett*

The Police Cop Man**

I'M the police cop man, I am, I am.
　Cars can't go till I say they can.
I stand in the middle of the street, I do,
And tell them to go when I want them to.
Whizzing taxis and automobiles,
Trotting horses and clattering wheels,
And rumbling, grumbling, huge big trucks,
And even the lazy old trolley car,
Can't go very far
　　When up goes my hand
　　　　　　and
　"Traffic stop,"
　　Says the traffic cop,
Then many little children's feet
Go hippity across the street.

—*Margaret Morrison*

*"The Green Bus" is from *I Go A-Traveling*, by James S. Tippett. By permission of Harper and Brothers, publishers.
**"The Police Cop Man" is reprinted from *Streets*, Cooperating School Pamphlet No. 2, by permission of the Bureau of Educational Experiments, 69 Bank Street, New York, and the John Day Company.

Biting Marion

LUCY SPRAGUE MITCHELL

ONCE there was a steam shovel. Her driver, Jim, called her "Biting Marion" because she was made at the Marion factory and because she loved to bite. She had an enormous square box, big enough to hold her engine. Her engine had many wheels and many belts. Round and round buzzed the wheels, and round and round glided the many belts when her engine was running.

She had a tall derrick, two stories high. Most exciting of all, she had an iron scoop with huge jaws that could open wide and bite into the earth. How Biting Marion loved to fill her great mouth with dirt. Dirt in her mouth, yum, yum! That was like candy to Biting Marion!

One day Jim, her driver, brought Biting Marion down a rough street all covered with heavy planks. She lurched and jolted along with the iron scoop at the top of the tall derrick swinging and bobbing. She moved slowly on funny long belts like broad steel chains that ran over and around the wheels. Jim sat in front of the engine in the big box and pulled a handle or turned a lever of the engine that told Biting Marion just what to do.

It told her to roll along close to a place where the workmen had taken up some of the heavy planks of the rough road and where the workmen had begun digging a hole. "Why do they want a hole in the street?" thought Biting Marion. But Jim knew the city was building a new subway. So he swung Marion's big derrick around until the scoop was over the hole in the street.

Reprinted from *Streets*, Cooperating School Pamphlet No. 2, by permission of the Bureau of Educational Experiments, 69 Bank Street, New York, and the John Day Company.

Jim made the big jaws open and Marion knew she was going to get her mouth full of delicious dirt. She began humming happily, "If they want me to eat, I'll eat the street; eat, eat, I'll eat the street." And down into the hole went the wide open jaws. She touched the dirt.

Then said Jim, "Now be polite and take a bite." Into the dirt she bit, gathering up dirt and stones into her huge iron mouth, mumbling:

"Eat, eat, I like to eat. Better than meat, I like the street to eat, to eat, to eat."

Jim moved another handle. Biting Marion closed her jaws on her delicious mouthful. "I'm Biting Marion, mighty Marion. I bite, I bite with all my might."

Another turn of another lever and up came the huge slobbering scoop, dirt and small stones drooling from the crack. Up, up, up and over until the scoop was just over a truck. "Now spit it out," murmured Jim. And Marion obediently opened up her big jaws again. Whang! came the dirt down into the truck. Bang! Whang!

Biting Marion was now quite happy. She was at the work she loved and to herself she softly sang,

> "Bite and spit,
> Bite and spit
> Until the hole's a great big pit.
> I'll make it deep,
> I'll make it steep
> With every bite and spit."

Jim in the big box was turning her again to the hole. The derrick was turned, the great jaws were open, the scoop was going down into the hole. "Bite," said Jim. "Be polite and take a bite." Biting Marion hummed her song, "Eat, eat, I like to eat. Better than meat, I like the street to eat, to eat, to eat."

Up again with the drooling, dribbling mouth, over the truck again, open the jaws again. And Biting Marion changed her tune.

"Bite and spit,
Bite and spit
Until the hole's a great big pit.
I'll make it deep,
I'll make it steep
With every bite and spit."

So Jim and Biting Marion worked to make the big hole for the city's new subway.

The Three Autos

LUCY SPRAGUE MITCHELL

THREE autos live in a big city.
The three autos are three different sizes—
    enormous
       big
       little.
The three autos are three different colors.
The enormous auto is painted brown.
The   big   auto is painted green.
The   little   auto is painted a bright, bright red.

All three autos go out on the city streets.
They go out in the sunshine.
They go out in the rain.
They go out in the snow.
On every kind of a day
    the three autos go out on the city streets.
The three autos live in three different houses.
The enormous auto lives in an enormous house.
The   big   auto lives in a   big   house.
The   little   auto lives in a   little   house.

Reprinted from *Streets*, Cooperating School Pamphlet No. 2, by permission of the Bureau of Educational Experiments, 69 Bank Street, New York, and the John Day Company.

The enormous brown auto
        goes out of its enormous house in the morning,
The big green auto
        goes out of its big house in the morning.
But the little red auto
        goes out of its little house
        any time in the day, or
        any time in the night.

The enormous brown auto carries lumber.
The   big   green auto carries meat.
But the little red auto carries the fire chief.

        The enormous auto goes fast on the city streets.
        The   big   auto goes faster still.
        But the little red auto goes the fastest of all.
        Like the wind, goes the little red auto.

    Listen!
    The autos are coming!

        Bump, bump,
            thump, thump,
        See the lumber jump inside the enormous brown auto!

            Rattle, rattle,
                clatter, clatter,
            See the meat baskets bounce inside the big green auto!

    Quick!
    Get out of the way!
    Up on the sidewalk!

        Quick!
        The little red auto is coming!

        Fast, fast!
        The little red auto is coming.
        The fire chief's auto is coming.

                Clang, clang,
                    Clang, clang,
                        Clang.

            Whew-eeeeeeeeeee-ew!

Train Story

IRMA SIMONTON

ONE day Henry and his mother went for a ride. What do you suppose they rode on? It wasn't an automobile nor a boat. It was something that was long and black, and it had an engine with many wheels and many cars behind it.

> Big and black
> It puffed down the track
> Pulling its many cars.

As it came, it said,

> "Chufchufchuf
> Chuf-chuf-chuf
> Chuf-chuf-chuf
> S-s-s-s-s-s-stop."

At the station, it puffed out smoke and a big bell said,

> "Dingdong, dingdong, dingdong, dingdong
> Must get along—must get along."

Reprinted from *Trains*, Cooperating School Pamphlet No. 4, by permission of the Bureau of Educational Experiments, 69 Bank Street, New York, and the John Day Company.

Then people came off the . . . train and went into the . . . station and all the people who were waiting in the station got on the train. Henry and his mother got on, too.

Then it started up

Chuf-chuf-chuf, slowly-slowly.
Chuf-chuf-chuf, faster-faster.

Then it went chufchufchuf-fastfastfastfast, as fast as it could go, to take Henry and his mother where they wanted to go.

Big and black
It puffed down the track
Pulling its many cars.

A Song of the Railroad Men

THE great Pacific railway,
   For California hail!
Bring on the great big engine,
Lay down the iron rail!
Across the rolling prairies
By steam we're bound to go;
The railroad cars are coming, humming,
Through New Mexico!

The little dogs in dog-town
Will wag each little tail;
They'll think that something's coming
A-riding on a rail.
The rattlesnake will show its fangs
The owl too-whit, too-whoo,
The railroad cars are coming, humming,
Through New Mexico!

Work gangs, building railroads, sang this song in the 1850's as they spiked rails to the ties. Roads from East and West were being pushed through plains and deserts and over mountains to meet triumphantly and link the whole country together.

Groceries

JAMES S. TIPPETT

THE store around the corner
    Has groceries to sell.
I go there with my mother;
I like that very well.

We look in the store windows
As we walk down the street.
We bring home many packages
Of groceries to eat.

Mister Postman

OLIVE BEAUPRÉ MILLER

HELLO there, Mr. Postman,
    I've been waiting here for you!
There's something, Mr. Postman,
That I want to say to you!

You bring my mother letters,
Daddy, too, and Auntie Bea.
Are you never, never thinking
That you should leave one for me?

With your pack all spilling over
Full of letters on your back,
You must have just one letter
For Miss Virjinjie Black!

M.S. HURFORD.

"Groceries" is from I Live in a City by James S. Tippett. By permission of Harper and Brothers, publishers.

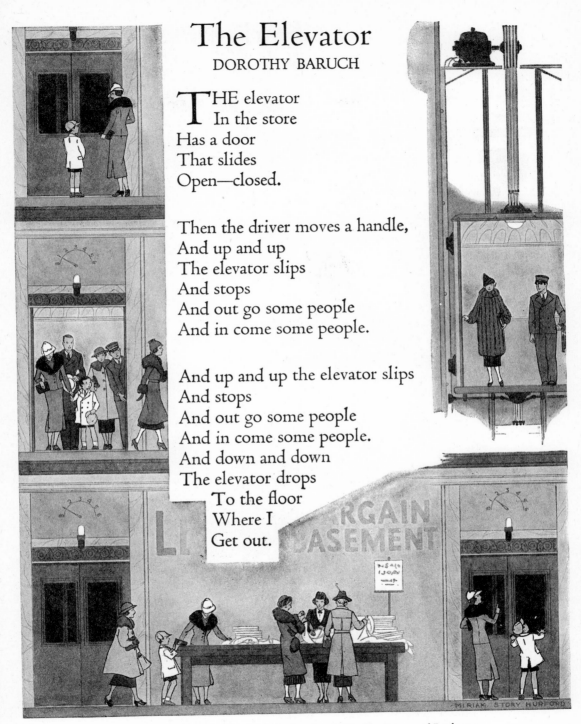

The Elevator

DOROTHY BARUCH

THE elevator
In the store
Has a door
That slides
Open—closed.

Then the driver moves a handle,
And up and up
The elevator slips
And stops
And out go some people
And in come some people.

And up and up the elevator slips
And stops
And out go some people
And in come some people.
And down and down
The elevator drops
To the floor
Where I
Get out.

From *I Like Machinery* by Dorothy Baruch, published by Harper and Brothers.

The Harbor

LOOK, see the boat!
Where? On the sea!
Swish through the waves it goes
Swish through the sea!

Look, see the smoke;
See its funnels red!
Hark, hear the whistle!
Woo-oo-oo! the whistle said.

—*Olive Beaupré Miller*

THE fog comes
on little cat feet.
It sits looking
over harbor and city
on silent haunches
and then moves on.*

—*Carl Sandburg*

*From *Chicago Poems.* Copyright by Henry Holt & Co.

Lines for a City Child

ROBERT AND ELIZABETH BROWNING

BANG-WHANG-WHANG, goes the drum,
    Tootle-te-tootle, the fife,
Oh, a day in the city square, there is no such
    pleasure in life!

—Robert Browning

GO out, children, from the mine and from the city;
    Sing out, children, as the little thrushes do;
Pluck your handfuls of the meadow cowslips pretty;
    Laugh aloud to feel your fingers let them through.

—Elizabeth Barrett Browning

The Zoo in the Park

HERE we go to the zoo in the park,
  The zoo in the park, the zoo in the park.
Here we go to the zoo in the park,
So early in the morning.

This is the way the elephant walks,
The elephant walks, the elephant walks.
This is the way the elephant walks,
So early in the morning.

This is the way the kangaroo hops,
The kangaroo hops, the kangaroo hops.
This is the way the kangaroo hops,
So early in the morning.

This is the way the monkey jumps,
The monkey jumps, the monkey jumps.
This is the way the monkey jumps,
So early in the morning.

This is the way the birdie flies,
The birdie flies, the birdie flies.
This is the way the birdie flies,
So early in the morning.

This game is sung to the tune of "Here We Go 'Round the Mulberry Bush." After circling
in a ring singing, children stand still and act out the movements of the animals in turn.

186

The Orchestra

OH, we can play on the big bass drum,
    And this is the music to it:
Boom, boom, boom, goes the big bass drum,
And that's the way we do it.

Oh, we can play on the violin,
And this is the music to it:
Fiddle-dee-dee, goes the violin,
And that's the way we do it.

Oh, we can play on the silver flute,
And this is the music to it:
Toot-toot-toot, goes the silver flute,
And that's the way we do it.

Oh, we can play on the big bass horn,
And this is the music to it:
Um-pah-pah, goes the big bass horn,
And that's the way we do it.

FERRING

Children join hands marching in a circle and singing. At the words, "And that's the way we
do it," they stand still and act out the motions of playing the musical instruments mentioned.

Sally's Blue Ball

MARIAN WALKER

SALLY had a new ball that was so big she had to hold it with her two hands. It was bright blue and it had two yellow stripes going around it.

Sally had a new ball,
A big ball, a blue ball
Sally had a new ball,
A ball with yellow stripes.

When it was time for Sally to go out of doors with her mother, she took her new ball with her. As she went down the steps, she dropped her blue ball and it went bumpety, bumpety, all the way down and rolled down the street. Sally called, "Oh, my new ball!" Just then the ball bumped against a baby carriage and stopped rolling. After that Sally held her ball tightly with two hands.

When Sally and Mother came to the park, Mother sat on a bench and Sally rolled her ball. She threw it toward a little hill. It went part way up and then rolled down. Sally ran after it and caught it. She threw the ball again and caught it when it rolled back to her. The next time she didn't catch it. It rolled down the path and bumped into a little boy. The little boy laughed and threw the ball back to Sally.

From *The Little Red Chair* by Marian Walker. By permission of The Macmillan Company, publishers.

Three times Sally rolled the ball far down the path and ran after it. Then she climbed up on the bench by her Mother and said, "Tell me a story." Mother told her about a little girl named Sally who had a big, bright blue ball with two yellow stripes going around it.

Sally had a new ball,
A big ball, a blue ball
Sally had a new ball,
A ball with yellow stripes.

Park Play

JAMES S. TIPPETT

EVERY morning
        I can play
In the park
Across the way.

I can run
And I can shout.
I am glad
    When I come out.*

*From I Live in a City, by James S. Tippett.
By permission of Harper and Brothers, publishers.

The Big Umbrella
and the Little Rubbers

ONCE there was a great big umbrella and once there was a little pair of rubbers. And the great big umbrella and the little pair of rubbers belonged to Barbara Ann. And in the house right next door to Barbara Ann's, there was a shiny black rain coat and a shiny pair of rubber boots. And the shiny black rain coat and the shiny black rubber boots belonged to a boy named Nickey.

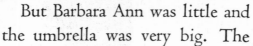

One day it began to rain, drip-drop, drippety-drop. So Barbara Ann's mother took the two little rubbers and put them on Barbara Ann. She opened the big umbrella, bang! And Barbara Ann took the umbrella and went out to walk in the rain. And Nickey's mother took the rubber boots and put them on Nickey and she took the shiny black rain coat and put that on Nickey, too. And Nickey went out in the rain. He went splish-splash in the puddles and squish-squash through the mud.

But Barbara Ann was little and the umbrella was very big. The umbrella was so very, very big it hid little Barbara Ann. All you could see of Barbara Ann was just her two little rubbers. Well, Nickey was playing around, splish-splish-splash in the rain when all of a sudden —look! What do you think he saw? He couldn't believe his own eyes. He ran in to his mother and said:

"Oh, Mother, come out and look! I just saw a great big umbrella and a little pair of rubbers go walking along up the street all alone by themselves!"

Rain

THE rain is raining all around,
  It falls on field and tree,
It rains on the umbrellas here,
And on the ships at sea.

—*Robert Louis Stevenson*

The Snow Man

ONE day, Robert woke up and the earth was all covered with snow like a great big white-frosted cake. The trees, the houses, and the bushes were all frosted white with snow. So Robert's Mother bundled Robert up all warm in his great big coat, his leggings, his thick cap, and his muffler. And Robert's Mother said:

*"Out we'll go
To see the snow
Till we take a tumble!"*

Then Robert's Mother put Robert on his sled and away they went into the yard. They slipped and slid around and they laughed and laughed and shouted. Crunch, crunch, crunch went Mother's feet and squeak, squeak went the sled as its runners slid along merrily over the fresh white snow.

By and by Robert's Mother began to roll up a big snowball. Robert got off his sled and Robert helped his Mother. When the first big snowball was done, Robert and his Mother rolled up another big snowball

and put it on top of the other. Then Mother ran away and came back with some coal. And Mother took the coal and she made two big black eyes, a nose, and a mouth in the face of the snowball. Then she put Father's old hat on top of it all. And there was a great, big snow man! Robert and his Mother shouted and shouted and laughed.

White Fields

IN the winter time we go
   Walking in the fields of snow;

Where there is no grass at all;
Where the top of every wall,

Every fence and every tree,
Is as white as white can be.

And our mothers always know,
By the footprints in the snow,

Where it is the children go.

—*James Stephens*

From *Collected Poems* by James Stephens, modern Irish poet and recorder
of Irish folk lore. By permission of The Macmillan Company, publishers.

The Airplane

AIRPLANE, airplane, up in the sky!
How I wish that I could fly!

Z-z-z, z-z-z, z-z-z! And burr-r, burr-r, burr-r!
Airplane, I hear you—purr-r, purr-r, purr-r!

If I were a bird, I know what I'd do!
I'd fly on my wings along with you!

—Olive Beaupré Miller

Thunder and Lightning

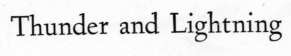

I LIKE the rain! I like the rain!
  It makes the world so clean!
The thirsty flowers, they drink it up—
I've watched them and I've seen!

I like the thunder, too, I do!
It makes so big a noise!
Rumble, grumble—*Bang!* it goes.
It makes more noise than boys!

And how I like the lightning flash!
Oh my, is that a sight!
To see a flash of lightning—bing!
Light all the world by night!

—Olive Beaupré Miller

Precocious Piggy

WHERE are you going to, you little pig?"
"I'm leaving my mother, I'm growing so big!"
"So big, young pig,
So young, so big!
What! Leaving your mother, you foolish young pig!"

"Where are you going to, you little pig?"
"I've got a new spade, and I'm going to dig."
"To dig, little pig?
A little pig dig!
Well, I never saw a pig with a spade that could dig!"

"Where are you going to, you little pig?"
"Why, I'm going to have a nice ride in a gig!"
"In a gig, little pig?
What! A pig in a gig!
Well, I never saw a pig ride in a gig!"

"Where are you going to, you little pig?"
"Well, I'm going to the ball to dance a fine jig!"
"A jig, little pig?
A pig dance a jig!
Well, I never before saw a pig dance a jig!"

"Where are you going to, you little pig?"
"I'm going to the fair to run a fine rig."
"A rig, little pig?
A pig run a rig!
Well, I never before saw a pig run a rig!"

"Where are you going to, you little pig?"
"I'm going to the barber's to buy me a wig!"
"A wig, little pig?
A pig in a wig!
Why, whoever before saw a pig in a wig!"
—Thomas Hood (1799-1845)

The Little Pig

THERE was once a little pig who lived with his mother. One day this little pig found that he had four little feet, and he cried out, "Wee, wee, big mother pig, what shall I do with my four little feet?" And big mother pig said, "Oof, oof, you funny little pig, you run with your four little feet." And the little pig ran round and round the barnyard.

One day the little pig found that he had two little eyes, and he said, "Wee, wee, big mother pig, what shall I do with my two little eyes?" And big mother pig said, "Oof, oof, you funny little pig, you look with your two little eyes." And the little pig looked and saw many, many things.

Then the little pig found that he had two little ears, and he said, "Wee, wee, big mother pig, what shall I do with my two little ears?" And big mother pig said, "Oof, oof, you funny little pig, you hear with your two little ears." And the little pig listened and heard many, many things.

By and by the little pig found his own little mouth, and he said, "Wee, wee, big mother pig, what shall I do with my one little mouth?" And big mother pig said, "Oof, oof, you funny little pig, you eat with your one little mouth."

At last the little pig found his one little nose, and he said, "Wee, wee, big mother pig, what shall I do with my one little nose?" And big mother pig said, "Oof, oof, you funny little pig, you smell with your one little nose."

Just then a little girl in a pink dress and white sunbonnet came down the lane carrying a pail in her hand. The little piggie listened with his two little ears, and heard her feet coming along the path. Then, with his two little eyes, he saw her pour something out of the pail into a trough. He ran very fast with his four little feet, and sniff, sniff, went his one little nose. "My, but it smells good!" said piggie; and, with his little mouth, he ate it all up.

THERE was a little boy went into a barn
  And lay down on some hay
A calf came out and smelt about
And the little boy ran away.

—*English Nursery Rhyme*

A Story of the Wind

JERRY was in his backyard. He was piling up sticks in his little red express wagon right beside the line where Tilda had hung out the clothes. All of a sudden Woo-oo— Jerry heard a noise. The dry leaves in the grass began to hop and flutter and fly around over the ground. Woo-oo! Woo-oo! Jerry knew that was the wind. He felt it blow hard on his face. The trees all started to shiver, to shiver and shiver and shake.

Woo-oo! Woo-oo! The wind went capering around until it came bolting down and filled all the clothes on the clothes line. Jerry's little nightie, Mother's and Tilda's dresses and Daddy's underwear, suddenly came to life. They danced and skipped and jumped and tugged away at the line. Zip, zip, rip! Jerry's little nightie pulled right away from the clothes line and flew off all by itself. And zip, zip, rip! Daddy's underwear pulled away from the clothes line, too, and chased after Jerry's nightie. They hopped on their queer little legs and popped right over the fence.

"Oh, oh, oh!" cried Jerry.

Woo-oo! Woo-oo! went the wind. Then, in another instant, the wind said nothing at all. The world was still as still. Jerry's little nightie and Daddy's underwear fell down flat on the ground. Tilda came out of the house, picked the runaways up, and hung them back on the line!

200

WHO has seen the wind?
   Neither I nor you;
But when the leaves hang trembling,
The wind is passing through.

Who has seen the wind?
Neither you nor I;
But when the trees bow down
   their heads,
  The wind is passing by.
         —Christina G. Rossetti

A Sea-Song from the Shore

JAMES WHITCOMB RILEY

HAIL! Ho!
　　Sail! Ho!
Ahoy! Ahoy! Ahoy!
　Who calls to me,
　So far at sea?
Only a little boy!

　　Sail! Ho!
　　Hail! Ho!
The sailor he sails the sea;
　I wish he would capture
　A little sea-horse
And send him home to me.

I wish, as he sails
    Through the tropical gales,
He would catch me a sea-bird, too,
    With its silver wings
    And the song it sings,
And its breast of down and dew!

I wish he would catch me a
    Little mermaid,
Some island where he lands,
    With her dripping curls,
    And her crown of pearls,
And the looking glass in her hands!

Children's Songs of Ancient Greece

HERE we come, we children come;
From door to door we sing!
See! We've found a swallow,
The first to come this Spring!

So give us something good to eat;
Give us cakes or cookies sweet;
Bring us bread, too, if you please;
And we'd like a piece of cheese!

Open the door! Open the door!
Take in the Swallow of Spring!
For we're no beggarmen out here;
We're only children who sing!

—*Theognis (500 B.C.)*

In Greece, 2500 years ago when children found the first swallow of Spring, they marched from door to door singing this song and hoping that those who heard them would give them gifts of cake or fruit or cheese.

CROCUS flowers bloom like fire;
  Narcissus drinks the rain;
And over all the hill-tops
Daffodillies bud again!

—*Melcager* (50 B.C.)

WHERE are my roses?
  Where are my violets?
    Where is my beautiful parsley?

These are my roses;
  These are my violets;
    This is my beautiful parsley!*

—*A Greek game, Athenaeus* (*Second Century, A.D.*)

*A children's game of ancient Greece. Historians think they advanced in two lines toward each other singing; then two children, one chosen from each side, joined right hands and each tried to pull the other across to his own ranks.

The Children and the Bear

ADAPTED FROM HANS CHRISTIAN ANDERSEN

ONCE a man had a big black bear. The bear could stand up on his hind legs and dance. And the man took him everywhere to dance for people. Well, one day he tied the bear to a tree and went into an inn to eat his dinner. By-and-by the bear got tired of staying outside alone. He broke loose from the tree and went into the inn. But he didn't see his master anywhere. So he pushed a door open with his paws. And there in the room before him he saw three children playing.

At first the children were afraid. They hid from him under a table. But the bear pattered over and sniffed at them in the friendliest way. So the little girl started to pat him. Then the bear lay down on the floor with his paws in the air as if he wanted the children to play with him. And the smallest boy threw himself down and rolled around on the floor with the bear. But the biggest boy got his drum. "Rub-a-dub!" he thumped on his drum. At that the bear stood up on his hind legs. Then the boy gave the bear a toy gun and he started to march like a soldier. So the other children got guns too. They all fell in line and

went marching like soldiers round and round the room.

They were having lots of fun when the children's mother came into the room. When she saw her children playing with that big black bear, her eyes opened wide. But the smallest boy laughed and said:

"Mother, we're all playing soldier!"

Just then the man came and took his bear away.

What They Say
MARY MAPES DODGE*

WHAT does the drum say? "Rub-a-dub-dub!
Rub-a-dub, rub-a-dub! Pound away, bub!
Make as much racket as ever you can.
Rub-a-dub! Rub-a-dub! Go it, my man!"

What does the trumpet say? "Toot-a-toot-too!
Toot-a-toot, toot-a-toot! Hurrah for you!
Blow in this end, sir, and hold me out, so.
Toot-a-toot! Toot-a-toot! Why don't you blow?"

What does the whip say? "Snaperty-snap!
Call that a crack, sir—flipperty-flap!
Up with the handle, and down with the lash.
Snaperty! Snaperty! Done in a flash!"

*Mary Mapes Dodge, as the editor of St. Nicholas over many years, was a favorite with children when Grandma was a girl. From Rhymes and Jingles. Copyright, 1874, by Scribner, Armstrong & Co.; 1904, by Charles Scribner's Sons.

It's Spring

THERE'S not a budding boy or girl this day,
But is got up and gone to bring in May.

—Robert Herrick

THE cock is crowing
The stream is flowing
The small birds twitter
The lake doth glitter
The green field sleeps in the sun!

—William Wordsworth

HEAR how the birds on every blooming spray
With joyous music wake the dawning day.

—Alexander Pope

May Day has been celebrated from the earliest times. In Rome, flower-decked processions honored Flora, goddess of flowers. In mediaeval Europe, people went a-maying carrying branches of trees and flowers and danced around a maypole.

GOOD MORROW, 'tis Saint Valentine's Day,
 All in the morning time,
And I a maid at your window,
 To be your Valentine.

—*William Shakespeare*

St. Valentine's Day has been celebrated since the 14th Century. As Shakespeare said: "Sweet lovers love the spring," and the festival of the Roman St. Valentine, on February 14, fell at a fitting time for lovers to send love missives.

Trip: San Francisco

LANGSTON HUGHES

I WENT to San Francisco
I saw the bridges high
Spun across the water
Like cobwebs in the sky.

Taken from *Golden Slippers*, a book of poems compiled by Arna Bontemps. Used by permission of the publishers, Harper and Brothers, and of the author, Langston Hughes, whose books of poetry include *The Negro Speaks of Rivers* and *The Dreamkeeper*.

Bats

by
EFFIE LEE NEWSOME

I'D really hate to go to bed
Just swinging from some wall.
But bats, they say, do just that way.
I'd not wish to at all.
I'd hate to swing down from my toes,
All upside-down, and try to doze.

From *Golden Slippers*, a book of poems compiled by Arna Bontemps. Used by permission of the publishers, Harper and Brothers, and of the author, Effie Lee Newsome. Among other books of poetry written by Effie Lee Newsome is *Gladiola Garden*.

What the Children Do in Summer

by

PEARL S. BUCK

THIS is what Michael likes to do in the summer. Michael likes to put on his bathing suit and jump into the pool. He likes to go down-down-down until the water is over his head. Then he pops up again and swims all around the pool. "I like to pop up," Michael says.

THIS is what Peter likes to do in summer. Peter likes to go down to the brook and take off his shoes and stockings and wade in the water and look for bright stones. He finds red ones and green ones and brown ones and yellow ones. "They are pretty stones," Peter says, and he keeps them in a box.

From *Stories for Little Children* by Pearl S. Buck, published by the John Day Company and used by permission of the author, Pearl Buck, the great American novelist, whose novels on China won for her in 1938 the Nobel prize for literature.

THIS is what David likes to do in the summer.
David likes to find wild strawberries hiding
in the grass. He picks them and eats them.
"I like the strawberries," David says.

THIS is what Barbara likes to do in the summer.
Barbara likes to take off her shoes and stockings and run in the grass. The grass is
cool and soft on her bare feet. She
laughs and laughs. "The grass
tickles my feet and makes
me laugh," Barbara says.

THIS is what Judy likes to do in the summer.
Judy likes to walk on the hill and pick
all the flowers she can find and put them
in her doll house for the dolls.
"The dolls like the
flowers," she says.

The Clucking Hen

"WILL you take a walk with me,
  My little wife, today?
There's barley in the barley field,
  And hayseed in the hay."

"Thank you," said the clucking hen;
  "I've something else to do;
I'm busy sitting on my eggs,
  I cannot walk with you."

The clucking hen sat on her nest,
  She made it on the hay;
And warm and snug beneath her breast
  A dozen white eggs lay.

Crack, crack, went all the eggs,
  Out dropped the chickens small;
"Cluck," said the clucking hen,
  "Now I have you all.

"Come along, my little chicks,
  I'll take a walk with you."
"Hello!" said the barn-door cock.
  "Cock-a-doodle-do!"
                    —*From Aunt Effie's Rhymes*

A Winky-Tooden Song

O HERE'S a little ryhme
   for the Spring or Summer-time—
An a-ho-winky-tooden-an-a-ho!
Just a little bit o' tune
   You can twitter, May or June,
An a-ho-winky-tooden-an-a-ho!

It's a lovely little thing
That 'most any one could sing
With a ringle-dingle-ding,
   Soft and low, don't you know,
An a-ho-winky-tooden-an-a-ho!
         —James Whitcomb Riley

From *Book of Joyous Children*, by James Whitcomb Riley, copyright 1902, 1930.
Used by special permission of the publishers, The Bobbs-Merrill Company.

Songs of Joy from The Bible

IT is God that hath made us and not we ourselves;
  For how great is his goodness and how great is his beauty!
    He hath made everything beautiful in his time.

He telleth the number of the stars;
He calleth them allby their names;

He covereth the heaven with clouds;
He prepareth rain for the earth;

He giveth snow like wool;
He hath blessed thy children within thee!

GOD hath made me to laugh
So that all that hear will laugh with me!
By my God have I leaped over a wall;
It is God that girdeth me with strength
And maketh my way perfect.

Mary and the Christ-Child
OLIVE BEAUPRÉ MILLER

FLOWERS are all a-blooming,
　Little birds do sing,
Mary's in the garden
Mid the flowers of spring.

Comes a shining angel
There beneath the tree.
"Mary," says the angel,
"Happy shalt thou be.

"Thou shalt have a baby,
Gentle, strong and mild;
God the Father giveth
Unto thee a child."

Mary Maiden answers:
"Great the joy you bring!
Unto God the Father
Joyfully I sing."

These pictures for *Mary and the Christ Child*, a subject which has inspired more beautiful pictures than any other, were suggested by the paintings of the Florentine artist, Fra Angelico, 1387-1455, who felt with childlike joy the beauty of the story.

Mary sings in springtime,
Sings in summer sun,
Waiting for the winter,
When the babe shall come.

Wisemen see the promise
In a shining star,
Come to greet the baby
Riding from afar.

Mary's husband, Joseph,
Says upon a day:
"We must go a journey
Far and far away."

The custom of singing carols to commemorate the birth of Christ goes back hundreds of years when children would go through the streets carrying lighted candles and singing lovely old songs such as *O Little Town of Bethlehem, Come All Ye Faithful*, etc.

Mary rides a donkey;
Joseph walks beside;
Over hill and valley
To Bethlehem they ride.

All the town is crowded;
Many people shout;
Roads are full of donkeys;
Camels all about.

Crowded, too, the inn is.
"Pray you, sir, a bed!"
Joseph asks for Mary
Place to lay her head.

"No rooms left tonight, sir;
You must go below;
Fresh clean stalls for cattle
There to you I'll show."

In the stable Mary
Lies at close of day;
Cows are gently lowing,
Camels chew the hay.

There that night to Mary
Is the Christ-child born;
Soon will bells be ringing
For the Christmas morn.

Joseph watches by her
While the babe they greet,
Lay him in a manger
Where the cattle eat.

Donkeys look in wonder;
Camels ope their eyes;
Cows behold the baby
In a slow surprise.

Shepherds on the hillside,
Watching flocks by night,
See a light a-shining,
Shining through the night.

Far away the shepherds
Hear an angel sing.
"Now is born the Christ-child!
Joy to earth I bring."

Hosts of angels answer,
Sing the song again;
"Unto God be glory!
Peace, good will to men!

"Joy the Christ-child bringeth!
Now is come to earth
Life and love and goodness
With the Christ-child's birth!"

Say the shepherds, "Come now,
Let us seek the child;
On his manger-cradle
All the angels smiled."

Shepherds seek the manger,
Find the baby there,
Find the babe with Mary,
Mary Mother fair.

Joseph stands beside her;
Donkey stands there too;
Little lambs are looking;
Cows are crying, "Moo!"

Bringing gifts, the Wise Men
In the doorway tread;
Shepherds kneel in wonder,
Shepherds bow the head.

Then they leave the manger,
Wandering to and fro;
Tell their happy tidings
Everywhere they go.

"O be glad, ye people!"
So the shepherds say;
"Lo, is born the Christ-child
Unto earth today!"

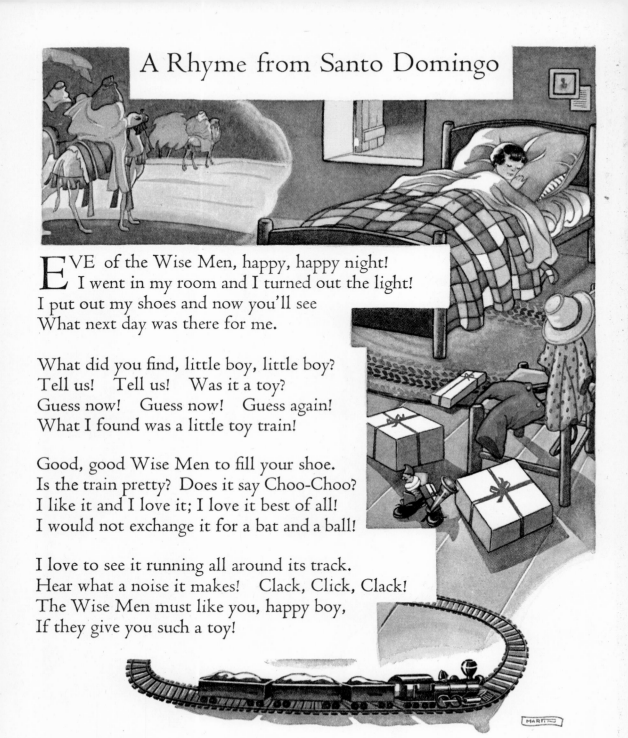

A Rhyme from Santo Domingo

EVE of the Wise Men, happy, happy night!
I went in my room and I turned out the light!
I put out my shoes and now you'll see
What next day was there for me.

What did you find, little boy, little boy?
Tell us!   Tell us!   Was it a toy?
Guess now!   Guess now!   Guess again!
What I found was a little toy train!

Good, good Wise Men to fill your shoe.
Is the train pretty? Does it say Choo-Choo?
I like it and I love it; I love it best of all!
I would not exchange it for a bat and a ball!

I love to see it running all around its track.
Hear what a noise it makes!   Clack, Click, Clack!
The Wise Men must like you, happy boy,
If they give you such a toy!

In Spain, Italy, and many Spanish-American countries presents are given to children on January sixth,
The Day of the Three Kings, commemorating the visit of the Wise Men to the Infant Jesus.